John Savage

Poems: Lyrical, Dramatic, and Romantic

John Savage

Poems: Lyrical, Dramatic, and Romantic

ISBN/EAN: 9783744787031

Printed in Europe, USA, Canada, Australia, Japan

Cover: Foto ©Andreas Hilbeck / pixelio.de

More available books at **www.hansebooks.com**

LYRICAL, DRAMATIC, AND ROMANTIC.

BY

JOHN SAVAGE.

NEW YORK:

JAMES B. KIRKER, PUBLISHER,

599 BROADWAY.

1867.

PREFACE.

In acceding to the Publisher's desire to embrace in one volume the works which form this collection, the author deems it a fitting opportunity to acknowledge that a paramount inducement to his doing so was found in a perusal of the reviews and criticisms called forth by these productions on their original appearance.

Of the thirty-seven pieces comprised in FAITH AND FANCY, thirty-two have been variously distinguished by "honorable mention" and commendatory criticism. SYBIL has met a favorable hearing in the study as well as upon the stage; and EVA, the latest published, if not so well known, is said by sufficiently high authority to be worthy of extended acquaintance. In a second edition of the first named (1864) some changes and corrections were introduced. In the present collection several verbal revisions are made.

The author will be pardoned for alluding with pride to the fact that the character of the criticisms referred to was in the ratio of the capacity of the writers. The most capable minds who noticed him were naturally the most discriminating and liberal in their remarks, while the few specimens of illiberality he met were portrayed with congenial flippancy and pretension.

It is an elevating consolation to the conscientious student—on whatever path—to know that while friendly criticism may not create lasting reputation, neither can unfriendly criticism prevent its achievement when deserved. If these pages contain the elements of poetic fire, truth, or beauty, they will live; if not, nothing can procure them a desirable longevity.

FORDHAM, November 21st, 1866.

TO

MRS. ELIZABETH A. SAVAGE,

WHOSE FORTITUDE UNDER SEVERE TRIALS,

SIMPLICITY OF CHARACTER AND STRENGTH OF AFFECTION,

HAVE MADE HER A GOOD MOTHER AND A CHEERING COMPANION,

This Collection

IS RESPECTFULLY AND AFFECTIONATELY DEDICATED

BY HER SON,

THE AUTHOR.

CONTENTS.

FAITH AND FANCY.

HON. CHARLES P. DALY, LL.D.,

MY DEAR FRIEND:

With great esteem for your many virtues and accomplishments, I dedicate this book of "Faith and Fancy" to you, and sincerely regret my inability to make it more worthy of your acceptance. While, however, I am thus proudly eager to let my readers know how I value private worth and public integrity; how in your person I honor purity of feeling, uprightness of character, and steadfast devotion to principle; and admire the variety of talent and intellectual resources which illustrate the unceasing promptings of your heart to generous efforts in behalf of Letters, Science, Humanity, and Justice;— while I thus take advantage of this Publication to boast sincere affection and respect for one so widely useful and so generally beloved, let me, under cover of the indulgence your public services will command, add a very few words touching the volume I offer you.

Prefaces, it would seem, are not so much the fashion now as in days gone by, though I am glad to see that some of our best and most powerful writers do not ignore the good old sociable custom. I confess to a feeling of self-respect which would compel me to raise my hat, by way of prefatory courtesy, to the person who, either at his own or my desire, was going to be the confidant of my hopes, woes, experiences, or sensations. Every person who writes poetry, is in such a position of self-exposure. If he aspire at all to transcribe or embody the feelings which evoke or prompt human action, he cannot help writing largely from his own heart's blood, and in the hues it has taken by contact with Men, Faith, and Nature. Hence, I desire to appropriate a paragraph of this dedicatory epistle to briefly convey to my kind readers what otherwise might be stated in a Preface.

With few exceptions, the pieces herein collected have been published—some anonymously and a few as translations—in various periodicals, during the past thirteen years; and in many instances received a degree of popular, and in some cases critical attention. I did not anticipate. After reproduction in various presses, some have found their way into collections; others have been read by professional readers to large and approving audiences; and others again—in the earlier portion of the volume—have been quoted by eminent and popular speakers on both sides of the Atlantic. The song at the opening of the Book, is placed there out of respect, not only to the subject which should be first in our hearts, but also to the gallant soldiers who gave it its first eclat on the historical occasion described in the note. However undue and unmerited the kind approbation referred to, *I* cannot overlook it; and in deeply appreciating it, feel some justification in collecting the scattered links of years between the Press, the Public, and myself; and—with the addition of a few others—welding all into a chain which, I trust, will bind me still more pleasantly and serviceably to them.

Begging you to receive this dedication as an humble though earnest tribute to good nature and great services,

I have the honor to be
Your friend and servant,
JOHN SAVAGE.

DECEMBER 13, 1868.

CONTENTS.

ρ

CONTENTS.

FAITH AND FANCY.

THE STARRY FLAG

Air—" *Dixie's Land.*"—*Recitativo.*

I.

Oh, the starry flag is the flag for me !
'Tis the flag of life ! the flag of the free !
   Then hurrah ! hurrah !
     For the flag of the Union !
      Oh, the starry flag, &c.

We'll raise that starry banner, boys,
   Hurrah ! hurrah !
We'll raise that starry banner, boys,
Where no power in wrath can face it.
   On town and field,
   The people's shield,
No treason can erase it !
   O'er all the land
   That flag must stand,
Where the people's might shall place it.

II.

That flag was won through gloom and woe!
It has blessed the brave and awed the foe!
Then hurrah! hurrah!
For the flag of the Union!
That flag was won, &c.

We'll raise that starry banner, boys,
Hurrah! hurrah!
We'll raise that starry banner, boys,
Where the stripes no hand can sever!
On fort and mast,
We'll nail it fast,
To balk all base endeavor!
O'er roof and spire
A living fire
The Stars shall blaze forever!

III.

'Tis the people's will, both great and small,
The rights of the States, the union of all!
Then hurrah! hurrah!
For the flag of the Union!
'Tis the people's will, &c.

We'll raise that starry banner, boys,
Hurrah! hurrah!
We'll raise that starry banner, boys,
Till it is the world's wonder!
On fort and crag
We'll plant that flag
With the people's voice of thunder!
We'll plant that flag
Where none can drag
Its immortal folds asunder!

IV.

We must keep that flag where it e'er has stood,
In front of the free, the wise, and the good !
    Then hurrah ! hurrah !
        For the flag of the Union !
            We must keep that flag, &c.

We'll raise that starry banner, boys,
    Hurrah ! hurrah !
We'll raise that starry banner, boys,
On field, fort, mast, and steeple !
    And fight and fall
    At our country's call,
By the glorious flag of the people !
    In God, the just,
    We place our trust,
To defend the flag of the people !

On board U. S. Transport " *Marion*," Monday, May 13, 1861.

THE MUSTER OF THE NORTH

A Ballad of '61.

I.

" Oh, mother, have you heard the news ?"
 " Oh, father. is it true ?"
" Oh, brother, were I but a man"—
 " Oh, husband, they shall rue !"
Thus, passionately, asked the boy,
 And thus the sister spoke.
And thus the dear wife to her mate,
 The words they could not choke.
" The news ! what news ?" " Oh, bitter news—they've
 fired upon the flag—
The flag no foreign foe could blast, the traitors down
 would drag."

II.

" The truest flag of liberty
 The world has ever seen—
The stars that shone o'er Washington
 And guided gallant Greene !
The white and crimson stripes which bode
 Success in peace and war,
Are draggled, shorn, disgraced, and torn—
 Insulted star by star ;

That flag which struggling men point to, rebuking kingly
    codes,
The flag of Jones at Whitehaven, of Reid at Fayal
    Roads."

III.

" Eh, neighbor, can'st believe this thing ?"
    The neighbor's eyes grew wild ;
Then o'er them crept a haze of shame,
    As o'er a sad, proud child;
His face grew pale, he bit his lip,
    Until the hardy skin,
By passion tightened, could not hold
    The boiling blood within ;
He quivered for a moment, the indignant stupor broke,
And the duties of the soldier in the citizen awoke.

IV.

On every side the crimson tide
    Ebbs quickly to and fro ;
On maiden cheeks the horror speaks
    With fitful gloom and glow ;
In matrons' eyes their feelings rise,
    As when a danger, near,
Awakes the soul to full control
    Of all that causes fear ;
The subtle sense, the faith intense, of woman's heart and
    brain,
Give her a prophet's power to see, to suffer, and main-
    tain.

V.

Through city streets the fever beats—
    O'er highways byways, borne—
2

The boys grow men with madness,
  And the old grow young in scorn ;
The forest boughs record the vows
  Of men, heart-sore, though strong ;
Th' electric wire, with words of fire,
  The passion speeds along,
Of traitor hordes and traitor swords from Natchez to
    Manassas,
And like a mighty harp flings out the war-chant to the
    masses.

VI.

And into caverned mining pits
  The insult bellows down ;
And up through the hoary gorges,
  Till it shouts on the mountain's crown ;
Then foaming o'er the table-lands,
  Like a widening rapid, heads ;
And rolling along the prairies,
  Like a quenchless fire it spreads ;
From workman's shop to mountain top there's mingled
    wrath and wonder,
It appalls them like the lightning, and awakes them like
    the thunder.

VII.

The woodman flings his axe aside ;
  The farmer leaves his plough ;
The merchant slams his ledger lids
  For other business now ;
The artisan puts up his tools,
  The artist drops his brush,

And joining hands for Liberty,
    To Freedom's standard rush ;
The doctor folds his suit of black, to fight as best he
        may,
And e'en the flirting exquisite is " eager for the fray."

VIII.

The students leave their college rooms,
    Full deep in Greece and Rome,
To make a rival glory
    For a better cause near home :
The lawyer quits his suits and writs,
    The laborer his hire,
And in the thrilling rivalry
    The rich and poor aspire !
And party lines are lost amid the patriot commotion,
As wanton streams grow strong and pure within the
        heart of ocean.

IX.

The city marts are echoless ;
    The city parks are thronged ;
In country stores there roars and pours
    The means to right the wronged ;
The town halls ring with mustering ;
    From holy pulpits, too,
Good priests and preachers volunteer
    To show what men should do—
To show that they who preach the truth and God above
        revere,
Can die to save for man the blessings God has sent down
        here.

X.

And gentle fingers everywhere
　　The busy needles ply,
To deck the manly sinews
　　That go out to do or die ;
And maids and mothers, sisters **dear,**
　　And dearer wives, outvie
Each other in the duty sad,
　　That makes all say " Good-by"—
The while in every throbbing heart that's pressed in fare-
　　well kiss
Arises pangs of hate on those who brought them all to
　　this.

XI.

The mustering men are entering
　　For near and distant tramps ;
The clustering crowds are centering
　　In barrack-rooms and camps ;
There is riveting and pivoting,
　　And furbishing of arms,
And the willing marching, drilling,
　　With their quick exciting charms,
Half dispel the subtle sorrow that the women needs must
　　feel,
When e'en for Right their dear ones fight the Wrong with
　　steel to steel.

XII.

With hammerings and clamorings,
　　The armories are loud ;
Toilsome clangor, joy, and anger,
　　Like a cloud enwrap each crowd ;

Belting, buckling, cursing, chuckling,
   Sorting out their " traps" in throngs ;
Some are packing, some knapsacking,
   Singing snatches of old songs ;
Fifers finger, lovers linger to adjust a badge or feather,
And groups of drummers vainly strive to reveille to-
    gether.

XIII.

And into many a haversack
   The prayer-book's mutely borne—
Its well-thumbed leaves in faithfulness
   By wives and mothers worn—
And round full many a pillared neck,
   O'er many a stalwart breast,
The sweetheart wife's—the maiden love's
   Dear effigy's caressed.
God knows by what far camp-fire may these tokens
    courage give,
To fearless die for truth and home, if not for them to
    live.

XIV.

And men who've passed their threescore years,
   Press on the ranks in flocks,
Their eyes, like fire from Hecla's brow,
   Burn through their snowy locks ;
And maimed ones, with stout hearts, persist
   To mount the belt and gun,
And crave, with tears—while forced away—
   To march to Washington.
     2*

"Why should we not? We love that flag! Great
    God!"—they choking cry—
"We're strong enough! We're not too old for our
    dear land to die!"

XV.

And in the mighty mustering,
  No petty hate intrudes,
No rival discords mar the strength
  Of rising multitudes ;
The jealousies of faith and clime
  Which fester in success,
Give place to sturdy friendships
  Based on mutual distress ;
For every thinking citizen who draws the sword, knows
    well
The battle's for Humanity—for Freedom's citadel!

XVI.

O, Heaven! how the trodden hearts,
  In Europe's tyrant world,
Leaped up with new-born energy
  When that flag was unfurled!
How those who suffered, fought, and died,
  In fields, or dungeon-chained,
Prayed that the flag of Washington
  Might float while earth remained!
And weary eyes in foreign skies, still flash with fire anew,
When some good blast by peak and mast unfolds that
    flag to view.

XVII.

And they who, guided by its stars,
    Sought here the hopes they gave,
Are all aglow with pilgrim fire
    Their happy shrines to save.
Here—Scots and Poles, Italians, Gauls,
    With native emblems trickt ;
There—Teuton corps, who fought before
    Für Freiheit und für Licht ;[2]
While round the flag the Irish like a human rampart go !
They found *Cead mille failthe*[3] here—they'll give it to
    the foe.

XVIII.

From the vine-land, from the Rhine-land,
    From the Shannon, from the Scheldt,
From the ancient homes of genius,
    From the sainted home of Celt,
From Italy, from Hungary,
    All as brothers join and come,
To the sinew-bracing bugle,
    And the foot-propelling drum :
Too proud beneath the starry flag to die, and keep secure
The Liberty they dreamed of by the Danube, Elbe, and
    Suir.

XIX.

From every hearth bounds up a heart,
    As spring from hill-side leaps,
To give itself to those proud streams
    That make resistless deeps !
No book-rapt sage, for age on age,
    Can point to such a sight

As this deep throb, which woke from rest
    A people armed for fight.
Peal out, ye bells, the tocsin peal, for never since the
        day
When Peter roused the Christian world has earth seen
        such array.

XX.

Which way we turn, the eyeballs burn
    With joy upon the throng ;
Mid cheers and prayers, and martial airs,
    The soldiers press along ;
The masses swell and wildly yell,
    On pavement, tree, and roof,
And sun-bright showers of smiles and flowers
    Of woman's love give proof.
Peal out, ye bells, from church and dome, in rivalrous
        communion
With the wild, upheaving masses, for the army of the
        Union !

XXI.

Onward trending, crowds attending,
    Still the army moves—and still :
Arms are clashing, wagons crashing
    In the roads and streets they fill ;
O'er them banners wave in thousands,
    Round them human surges roar,
Like the restless-bosomed ocean,
    Heaving on an iron shore :
Cannons thunder, people wonder whence the endless river
        comes,
With its foam of bristling bay'nets, and its cataracts of
        drums.

XXII.

"God bless the Union army!"
  That holy thought appears
To symbolize the trustful eyes
  That speak more loud than cheers
"God bless the Union army,
  And the flag by which it stands,
May it preserve, with freeman's nerve,
  What freedom's God demands!"
Peal out, ye bells—ye women, pray; for never yet went
      forth
So grand a band, for law and land, as the muster of the
      North.

THE PATRIOT MOTHER.

I.

When o'er the land the battle brand
  In freedom's cause was gleaming,
And everywhere upon the air
  The starry flag was streaming,
The widow cried unto her pride,
  " Go forth and join the muster ;
Thank God, my son can bear a gun
  To crown his race with lustre !
Go forth ! and come again not home,
  If by disgrace o'erpowered ;
My heart can pray o'er hero's clay,
  But never clasp a coward !"

II.

"God bless thee, boy, my pride, my joy,
  My old eyes' light and treasure—
Thy father stood 'mid flame and blood
  To fill the freeman's measure.
His name thy name—the cause the same,
  Go join thy soldier brothers !
Thy blow, alone, protects not one,
  But thousands, wives and mothers.
May every blessing Heaven can yield
  Upon thy arms be showered !
Come back a hero from the field,
  But never come a coward."

SOLDIER'S SONG.

I.

I'D rather be a soldier
In a gallant, glorious cause,
To uphold a people's honor,
Their liberty and laws,
Than wearily and drearily
To pass my life away,
Living but for living's sake,
And dying ev'ry day.

Chorus.—I'd rather be a soldier !
A tramping, camping soldier !
A soldier away to the field
Where the God of right above,
Smiles upon the flag we love,
As we fight, fall, but never yield.

II.

I'd rather be a soldier
In the watchful bivouac,
'Mid night alarms, and calls to arms,
To meet the dawn's attack,
Than slumber in the city's heart,
In callous, blank repose,

When every man should be awake
To face the nation's foes.

I'd rather be a soldier, etc.

III.

I'd rather be a soldier,
In the flashing, crashing van,
And win the love of mankind,
By the blow I strike for man,
Than mope in subtle selfishness,
With empty pleas for " Peace,"
While each delay to win the right
But makes the wrong increase.

I'd rather be a soldier, etc.

IV.

I'd rather be a soldier,
'Mid the battle's rage and ire,
With heart that mocks the sabre thrust,
And soul that scoffs the fire,
Than live to feel no glory
In my nation, flag, and race—
Oh, better fall to crown them all,
Than live to their disgrace !

I'd rather be a soldier, etc.

V.

Then forward, gallant comrades !
Welcome any fate that comes ;
We rise to freedom's bugle-blast,
We step to freedom's drums :

The God that gave us liberty,
 Will see us through the foam
Of battle, while we bravely fight
 For our dear ones at home.

I'd rather be a soldier, etc.

2

GOD PRESERVE THE UNION.

I.

Brothers, there are times when nations
  Must, like battle-worn men,
Leave their proud, self-builded quiet
  To do service once again :
When the banners blessed by fortune,
  And by blood and brain embalmed,
Must re-throb the soul with feelings
  That long happiness hath calmed.
Thus the Democratic faith that won
  The nation, now hath need
To raise its ever stalwart arm,
  And save what twice it freed.

        So friends fill up
        The brimming cup
    In brotherly communion—
        Here's blood and blow
        For a foreign foe,
    And God preserve the Union.

II.

There are factions passion-goaded,
  There are turbulence and wrath,
And swarthy dogmas bellowing
  Around the people's path ;

There are false lights in the darkness,
  There are black hearts in the light,
And hollow heads are mimicking
  The Jove-like people's might.
But, ah! the Democratic strength
  That smote an empire's brow,
Can with its regnant virtues tame
  Mere home-made factions now.

      So friends let's band
      For fatherland—
   In brotherly communion,
      Let every mouth
      Cry " North and South,"
  And God preserve the Union.

III.

While the young Republic's bosom
  Seems with rival passions torn—
Growing from the very freedom
  Of the speech within it born ;
Europe, in its haggard frenzy
  To behold no earthly sod,
Where its white slaves may unbend them,
  Or bend but to Freedom's God—
Europe madly hails the omen—
  Strains its bloodshot eyes to view
A native treason toiling at
  The work it strove to do.

      So, friends, let's all
      Like a rampart wall—
   In granite-built communion,

> Stand firmly proud,
> 'Gainst the kingly crowd—
> And God preserve the Union.

IV.

Since that day, when frantic people
   Round the State House rose and fell,
Like an angry ocean surging
   Round some rock-reared citadel—
When the Quaker City trembled
   'Neath the arming people's tramp,
And the bell proclaimed to iron men
   Each house in the land a camp—
Democracy has kept that bell
   Still pealing sound on sound,
Until its potent energy
   Has throbbed the wide earth round.

> So let it ring,
> So let it bring
> Us brotherly communion ;
>   Here's heart and hand,
>   For life and land !
> And God preserve the Union !

A BATTLE PRAYER.

I.

God of the righteous, God of the brave!
Strengthen our arms our country to save ;
Lead us to victory's peace-giving charms :
God of the righteous, strengthen our arms!

II.

God of the people's cause, God of the free !
From hearth and hill-side we look up to Thee ;
Make us, when battle-clouds thunder and roll,
Titans in body, and true men in soul.

III.

God of our hopefulness, God of the right !
Be to us armor and courage in fight !
Lift us on valorous fervor to be
Terror and wrath to the foes of the free !

IV.

God of humanity, God of the heart!
Let not the man in the soldier depart ;
And when beneath us the ruthless foe reels,
Teach us the mercy the true hero feels.

3*

v.

Gird up our loins then, O Lord! for the truth,
The safety of age, and the freedom of youth;
Leads us to victory's peace-giving charms:
God of the righteous strengthen our arms!

REQUIEM FOR THE DEAD OF THE IRISH BRIGADE.

COME, let the solemn, soothing Mass be said,
For the soldier souls of the patriot dead.

Let the organ swell, and the incense burn,
For the hero men who will ne'er return.

Men who had pledged to this land their troth,
And died to defend her, ere break their oath.

But if high the praise, be as deep the wail
O'er the exiled sons of the warlike Gael.

From their acts true men may examples reap ;
And women bless them, and glórýing, weep.

Proud beats the heart while it sorrowing melts
O'er the death-won fame of these truthful Celts.

For the scattered graves over which we pray
Will shine like stars on their race alway.

Oh, what doth ennoble the Christian man,
If not dying for truth in freedom's van !

What takes from Death all its terrors and gloom ?
Conscience to feel Justice blesses the tomb !

And oh! what doth build up a nation's weal
But courage to fight for the truths we feel !

And thus did these braves, on whose graves we wait,
Do all that make nations and races great.

OREMUS.

Ye living, your hearts combine
In praise and prayer, to the heavenly shrine :
Ye widowed and stricken,
Your trustfulness quicken
With faith in the Almighty Giver ;
And may blessed repose
Be the guerdon of those
Who fell at Antietam and James's river,
By the Rappahannock and Chickahominy ;
Requiem æternam dona eis, Domine !
May their souls on the Judgment-day arise ;
Et lux perpetua luceat eis.

REDEMPTION.

" A sound heart is the life of the flesh."—Proverbs.

I.

MISER, see that hoard of gold—
    Mistress, view that dower—
Artist, look at yon fair mould—
    Beauty, wealth, and power :
There they are—but what are these ?
False leaves decking sapless trees.

II.

Honesty for *him* hath naught—
    Truth for *her* no use—
Yon fair shape no virtue brought—
    All are life's abuse :
But like Christ, one pure heart's birth
Brings redemption to an earth !

FLOWERS ON MY DESK.

Ye tiny queens, lift up your pensive heads,
And fear not that a magic feeling weds
The air about the student's chamber;
  'Tis true these books inoculate the air
  With their intense divinity,
  And measure in the rhythm of each mystic prayer
  The hopes and blessings of infinity:
But ye may into all their secrets clamber,
  As little stars may wander through the skies,
  And find out all the bliss of Paradise.

  The poet and the plant are near allied;
  Nature's best offspring, she of both the pride:
  So, fear thee not, nor fail to number,
  Amongst thy friends those stately quartos which—
Some standing upright to their proudest height,
And some reclining in a tired plight,
  Like drows-eyed sentinels who laz'ly hitch
  Their sides to wakeful slumber—
Gather around as if to guard the prize,
That dainty hands and brightest eyes
Had culled for me.   Ye conjure up
    Like the swift shadow of a welcome comer,
    Or early buds that whisper us of summer—
You fragrant rose and rustic buttercup,

The pleasant presence of the picturesque,
    And light and artless,
    But dare I say the heartless
Maid, who gave you to my musty desk.

    Like her, you're fair,
      And like her, too, you're tender,
    Light as May air,
      Commingled with June splendor,
Joyous as Morning when he freshly gives
    A like rich mirth
To all around that in his radiance lives
    In air or earth ;
And which we love to foster as we stray,
    While yet the town
Winks doubtful welcome to the god of day,
    In midnight's gown.

Ah ! I can picture how she tripped amid
   The little fay-ground where she tends her flowers,
To woo ye, as ye childishly all hid
   Each others' smile, love-chained to natal bowers ;
Yes, I can picture how she tripped along,
   Her clear laugh car'lling on the jealous air,
Which, though unquiet, calmed to catch her song,
   And test its fragrance with her wild breath there.

And then she, heedless of the list'ning vapors,
   Footed around to cull the richest stems,
Here eyes a plant, then onward gayly capers,
   And here again, and there, for perfume gems ;
Now choosing one, and now discarding ten,
   The while those ten grow ripe her love-light quaffing.

And now she plucks a dainty pair, and then
　Her young and happy heart is wildly laughing.

My dainty flowers, dwell ye on my desk,
　Among my choicest friends, and dear good-fellow books
Dwell there to memorize the picturesque,
　And laughing, bright-eyed, fairy-tinted looks
　Of her who culled you from your fragrant nooks
　　　In her self-tended Eden :
　　　In your glee—
　Dwell, tender queens, to picture forth the maiden
　　　Who gave you unto me.

How rich a thing becomes the merest leaf,
When memories—that give the mind relief—
Of love, of hope, ay even, or of grief,
Are twined in fragrant bondage to it!
What various raptures whirl us as we view it?
Each rapture leaping up from thought's horizon,
Like the rich clouds that fleck the ambient skies on
Summer days between the noon and even—
Golden and fantasque, sailing through bright heaven
As richest thoughts through god-like poet's brain ;
The music of whose full-toned purple strain
Will be cast back from every cone of thought
That leaps delighted with the soul thus brought
Into its lesser being, lighting some lesser still,
Until wide prairies of reflected will
Send up, like exhalations from the vernal
　Sun-besmitten and inspired sod,
Their thanks which make the poet's dreams eternal.
　The poet does not *dream*—he *lives* with God,
Who is the essence of all right and beauty—

He does *not* dream, but lives a life of duty,
So far above "realities" of Earth, that Earth
   With mind, like dagger to a point grown thin
In peculation, will not see his worth,
   But calls his life a dream to shield its lifelong sin.
And as I gaze on yon sweet leafy links
Of thought, my too unguarded Fancy drinks
Whole stoups of Hope, that frolic through *my* brain
Like summer clouds in Evening's calm domain ;
And they too like the poet's thoughts send back
Reflected glory on their founder's track.

While ye remain there I shall think it Night,
   Night calmly eloquent and grand ;
And ye the lamps that shed their vesper light
   In the dim cloisters of the poet's land ;
And when ye fade, I'll feel the silence parted,
   And Day, hot-headed, panting in my face,
With words too broken for the gloomy-hearted
   To hang a hope on for his spirit's grace.

4

A PHANTASY.

I was dreaming, the other night, over my desk,
　　　　All alone,
And my thoughts held me still in a net arabesque
　　　　Of my own ;
And, as Joy at its height held in silence, I sat,
　　　　When a chord
My soul's yearning portals there came ringing at,
　　　　And I heard
A peal of sweet maid-laughing tones : and I listened
　　　　And gazed ;
When out from the silence a pair of eyes glistened !
　　　　I raised
My hands to my eyes, which felt doubtful of vision.
　　　　Forbear,
Ye Gods of the Fancy ! what features elysian
　　　　Were there !
An eye, bright as Spring after kissing the rain,
　　　　And a voice,
With the richness of Psyche's and Flora's wild strain,
　　　　Did rejoice !
And leaped its sweet carols my poor heart a-through,
　　　　From a mouth
Rich as strawberry juice, or the rose 'neath the dew
　　　　In the South !
And her form bright as hope, seemed to beckon me on,

And the power
Of my own language came, and I spoke . . . all was gone
Save a flower.

. . . .

Why Fancy—why Beauty—whatever thou art,
Dost thou chain,
Promethean like, to the rock of my heart
My wild brain?
Oh, tender soul, tell me what likeness thou'lt rear,
In *thy* power,
'Tween a love-laughing sprite of a maiden so fair
And a flower?

MINA.

I.

Mina's eyes are dark as sorrow,
Mina's eyes are bright as morrow—
    Morrow symbols Hope alway;
And a soul-lit radiance flashes
Out between their silken lashes,
As from out the sable fringes of the midnight leaps the
    day.

II.

Mina's hair is black as madness,
Mina's hair is soft as gladness—
    Gladness true is soft and low;
And its heavy richness ponders
O'er her brow, as student wanders
By some bardic temple, wordless with the homage he'd
    bestow.

III.

Mina's brow is clear as amber,
Mina's brow is calm as chamber
    Where God lives in what seems dead;
And its gentleness is giving
E'er a mute excuse for living
On in passive grandeur, careless of the fame its thoughts
    might spread.

IV.

Mina's mouth is ripe as study,
Mina's mouth is full and ruddy—
  Tempting as the August peach ;
And its sweet contentment routing
Off a melancholy pouting,
Welcomes laughter to the portals where the trivial ne'er
  can reach.

V.

Mina's heart is pure as childhood,
Mina's heart is fresh as wildwood,
  Where each tendril dials God ;
And its radiant blessings centred
On her face, have ever entered
Through her eyes those happy mortals who within their
  mission trod.

VI.

Mina's hand is sure to capture !
Mina's touch is weird—its rapture
  Is electric, seeming numb ;
And her spirit on the minute
Thrills you with the calm joy in it,
And vibrating you to eloquence, compels you to be dumb.

   4*

"REMEMBER WE ARE FRIENDS."

"No matter what comes about, our friendship must not be severed."

I.

REMEMBER we are friends, dear girl, though far apart and
    lonely,
And though the sunlight of your smile is now a mem'ry
    only—
And though the love I dreamed my own is tombed
    where sorrow blends
The hopings of the stormy past—remember we are
    friends !

II.

Mayhap you'll feel the ocean world too chill, your life-
    shore beating—
Mayhap your heart, like mine, may see its darling hope
    retreating—
God grant you joy !—but who may know what comes
    when daylight ends ?
And should e'er morrow bring you gloom—remember
    we are friends.

III.

And though I'd prize your love beyond all womanly
    affection,
And though a hope will linger yet to feed my heart's
    dejection,

I'd rather have thy young heart blessed, in blessing
    where it bends—
Forget me as a lover, but—remember we are friends !

IV.

I'll meet thee yet beside the hearth—that hearth that i
    another's,
And my still young gray hairs shall joy o'er faces like
    their mother's !
Mayhap *he'll* twit my loneliness, and boast what marriage
    sends,
Unknowing how I once thought, but—remember we are
    friends.

TO AN ARTIST.

THE old man's drifted to the soundless sea—
  Gone back to earth and heaven : as a perfume, he
Warmed into life by light rose into sky's immensity.

  Blondell, I have to thank thee, and thy art
  For every tremor that awakes my heart
From gloom, when gazing on his pictured counterpart.

  Your pencil's magic drew up to his face
  His innate radiances, as the sunlight's grace
Makes voluble the innate seed in flowers on earth's placid
    space.

  His fair round forehead, like a concave glass,
  Enlarged all good it witnessed to a mass,
The convex lessening ill, so that none ever saw it pass.

  His kind, love-typifying face is here
  With all its fond intensity ; it would appear
The great old man himself had just but ceased to rear

  The vocal solace of his thoughts around,
  And dropped off into silence, while the sound
Of his own blessed words yet o'er his features wound :

Ay, in the lustre of their purity,
As noiseless mists about a fountain's glee
Hover on the air, and then in wavy sun-bows flee.

Like some great diver, you have made a bound
Into his nature, loving, vast, profound,
And scattered o'er the canvas the gems profuse you
    found.

He was the sun that lit my childhood on,
And smiled upon me as on earth the sun ;
But now your canvas, like a moon, reflects the light that's
    gone.

But on my morn no Sun shall say to Earth
" God bless you !" as oft he : his song, his mirth
Have gone with evening and the birds—all here is voice-
    less dearth.

I cannot weep, I have such stupor drank ;
Enough, like sunless day I am all blank ;
He left me drunk with Love, and guideless have I sank.

All his quaint humors, all his cheering sense,
Ghost through my brain, that, vague with wild intents
Grasps at them all, and finds but shadowy cerements.

A thousand questions crowd upon my tongue,
With thousand answers springing them among ;
For he was of me, and his thoughts like mantles o'er me
    hung.

Mankind lost more than I did when he plied
  His soul's white wings for heaven—though my pride
And guide left me and mine unsolaced when he died.

God's noblest work evanished when he fled,
  This great world missed an honest man's meek tread
The hour it opened to receive my father's body—DEAD.

Sept. 23, 1853.

LILLA.

I.

Lovely Lilla, why keep smiling?
All my path to gloom beguiling;
As your mouth its bright joy flashes,
Every ripple o'er me dashes—
Makes me helpless while I gaze on
Nature's acted diapason;
But the bliss a bane instills—
Lilla smiles while Lilla kills.

II.

Ah! those eyes with rapture thrill me—
Take them off, or else they'll kill me;
But not yet, for there's about them
That to make me die without them!
Dear, remember what you're doing,
You are killing while I'm wooing—
If you close those eyes of blue,
Don't you know you close mine too?

III.

Such an earthly, heavenly, human,
Lovely, wicked, artless woman

As you, Lilla, lights our blindness
Rarely here, to kill with kindness !
Every glance both wins and wounds me—
Life or Death in you surrounds me—
While one word *all* life would give,
Had you the heart to make me live.

HAUNTED.

I AM haunted by a spirit,
  Everywhere I go ;
That I'm near it, yet not near it,
  I too sadly know.

When I'm hushed and sorrow-laden,
  'Tis a solace there ;
When my heart would clasp its maiden
  Figure—it is air.
Now deluded, now hope-nurtured—
  I am cursed and blessed,
Till I crave for this o'er-tortured
  Frame, eternal rest.

Yet the spirit looms about me,
  Like a thought decreeing,
As I from it—it without me—
  Cannot have a being.

I am in the city's mazes,
  'Mid ten thousand men—
There the spirit's sweet, sad face is
  Smiling, just as when,
In the midnight, it from study
  All my soul has drawn ;

5

Or when it, at morning ruddy,
        Smiles a rival dawn.

Sometimes it is sad and lonely—
        Sometimes like a psalm,
A sacred, solemn joy—this only
        When *I'm* very calm ;
Sometimes 'tis as bright as dew, that
        Pushed from opening bud,
Steals the light it first falls through, that
        Gilds it ere it kiss the sod ;

Sometimes 'tis a gloomy grandeur—
        Sorrow unconfessed—
Whose loud silence would command your
        Life to calm its breast ;

Sometimes smiling as a dreaming
        Child—the thoughts, alas,
Of the soul on lips are beaming
        That they cannot pass ;
Sometimes—but, O heart, some feature
        Bless in silent prayer !
All times seeming—'tis some creature
        Rare, exceeding fair !

So, two shadows' dim distraction
        Dial every motion ;—
One, which guides my body's action,
        One, my soul's devotion.

LOVE'S IMAGINATION.

I.

WHERE the mist is list'ning
   To the stoic hills,
Where the spray is glist'ning
   O'er the joyous rills,
Where the budding flowers
   Nodding by the streams,
Look like infants waking
   From their rosy dreams;
There may hearts grow fonder,
There may poet ponder,
There may fancy squander,
   All its jewels rare,
But there I may not wander
   If my love's not there.

II.

Where the tall pines shiver,
   When the winter's breath
Wraps the once glad river
   Into icy death;
Where the caverns labor
   With a restless pray'r,

When the hunted ocean
   Seeks a shelter there;
There, though desolation,
Mocks all contemplation,
Love's imagination
   Mellows place and time,
And in its own creation
   Makes the gloom sublime !

"MAY GOD BLESS US.'

I.

LADY mine, say it ever, pray it ever, it hath meaning,
For the lowly, for the holy, and to all on virtue leaning,
But from *thy* lips to *me* it hath a hope all else above,
For God *is* love, and truly blesses those who truly love.

II.

Love's the secret of existence ! What are vineyards—
    spacious portals—
To one happy tear, one honest blush, that blends two
    trusting mortals ?
Oh, he's infidel, who loves not, to himself and God above,
For God is love, and truly blesses those who truly love.

CELIA'S TEA.

CELIA makes such brain-enlivening tea,
    That when one's ta'en the draught celestial up,
He feels so happy, that it oft struck me,
    She must have poured her heart into the cup.

5*

A NEW LIFE.

I.

Is it fancy, am I dreaming,
　　Do I tread the realms of faery—
Do my hopings mock my wild heart with the echoes of
　　　　itself ;
　　Is my soul lit by the beaming
　　　　Of your radiant face, fair Lilla ?
Or, am I witched, like pilgrim, by the lagoon's midnight
　　　　elf ?

II.

　　Sweet words are singing o'er me,
　　And beside me and before me,
Yet I fear to think them truthful, lest I wake to find me
　　　　wrong;
　　And the bliss of the first minute,
　　When my heart caught them within it,
Would woo me to eternal sleep, to ever dream such song.

III.

　　God is loving—God is jealous,
　　　　And we're every mortal fashioned
In the likeness of the Moulder ! and our sympathies so
　　　　bent,

Can my words be over zealous,
    Or my love be too impassioned?
No, I cannot outstrip nature, though I fail to be content.

IV.

I have had my dreams of glory,
    And have quaffed my youthful chalice—
What bitter dregs lay thickening underneath its starry
    foam?
And my life broke, like the story
    Of that oriental palace,
Whose magic marble fabric sank, and left no trace of
    home.

V.

In my thoughts' dim, lonely prison,
    Where I dwelt, a voice has risen,
As the angel's unto Peter, giving comfort, hope, and
    cheer;
And so full of light's the tremor,
    It now pulses through the dreamer,
He'd bless the thought that chains him to have that
    angel near.

VI.

Was your heart so sympathetic
    That it caught *my* words unspoken,
As they welled up, seeking utterance love-confused to
    very fear?
Was it you that said " I love thee"—
Was it I that said " I love thee ;"
Or, did we each the other's heart unburden to the ear?

VII.

When you twined your arms about me
Saying life was dark without me—
That *I* was the one comforter you prayed of God to
give—
That among the thousands fleeing
Past, you knew me as *that* being;
My heart, beneath the revelation, paused to say "I live!"

VIII.

There's a strange new life upon me,
With a clarion-toned suffusion
Of joy, that cannot sound itself with words of mortal
speech;
But it is no fancy won me,
No mere student-bred delusion;
'Tis thy vatic words that make a dual future in my reach.

IX.

What a bounteously decreeing
Gift hath love, when it receiving
Love for love, transfigures us to things undreamed be-
fore?
Now I've two lives in my being,
You have two lives in your living,
And yet we have but one dear life between us evermore.

THE GOD-CHILD OF JULY

A Birth-day Ode.

On the middle day of the middle month
   Of the heavenly-fashioned summer,
When vines were scaling the antique eaves,
And earth lay in shade under motionless leaves,
     And the sap of the sod,
     By the blessing of God,
Ran leaping and romping through branch-woven bowers,
Was tittering in tendrils and laughing in flowers :
Like young happy children love-linked to each other,
     Who spring from to brighten,
     And clinging to lighten,
With ever fresh pride, the rich breast of their mother.

In such a midday of the middle month
   Of the golden-dowered summer,
My better angel was sent from above,
Born to the Earth with her mission of love ;
And Earth, with the favors of rich July,
   Arrayed the gentle comer.

The mingled radiance of the illumined space
     Centred on her face,
     With the blue of the skies
     Were tinct her eyes,

And the staid and holy air
Filled her with prayer ;
The fruitage of the Earth
Gave her ripe mirth,
And the myriad floral dyes
Numberless shades of pleasantries ;
The mighty oak outstretched its arms at length,
Standing strong sponsor for her strength,
And the trustful vine
Taught her to entwine
Her soul around the strong to beautify it :
The conscious heat of noon lent her full power to defy it

The freshened dawn, in night-escaped security,
Thrilled her fresh heart with clarion tones of purity :
The evening breeze
Brought her revivifying ease ;
The half-parched streams, with mutual assistance,
Made a flush river to teach her mind persistence ;
And crowds of wealthy humble bushes quaint
Gave her their unambitious birthright—self-restraint.
The ash upon the mountain's rugged side
Told her in life and liberty to pride ;
And the yew, bending its melancholy head,
Taught her to weep the dead.
The wild plants of the wood
Showed her the weal of solitude,
And preached of modesty in their fresh enamels ;
The lightning, leaping from its ebon trammels,
Showed her, as it unfurled,
The electric lord and servant of the world.
The rapid thunder, that in hot July
Strikes earth with all the ordnance of the sky,

Rolled its unseen artilleries
Through the black gorges of those weird cordilleras
 Of cloud which mock imagination—
Poured its mysterious majesty of sound
The god-child of its favored month around,
 And woke the drowsy day to hearty acclamation

Ah me, so tended was this tender creature
Within by heavenly, without by earthly nature,
She grew a being strong without alloy,
To bless in sorrow, to sustain in joy—
In wealth be calm, in poverty be rich,
Until one questioned with her which was which.
Within the world, she is so much above it
She lessens not herself, nor it to love it ;
With faith surrounding, leading all things human,
At once a loving wife and trustful woman.

The anniversary of her natal day
Is rung, by the chimes, to the times passed away.

I pray of Heaven, which has vouchsafed to me
The guardianship of such condensed variety
As the dear Past, to let the Future be
Suffused with Love, sublimed by Piety

July 15th.

BREASTING THE WORLD.

I.

MANY years have burst upon my forehead,
 Years of gloom and heavy freighted grief;
And I have stood them as against the horrid
 Angry gales, the Peak of Teneriffe.

II.

Yet if all the world had storm and sorrow,
 You had none, my better self, Lenore,
My toil was as the midnight seeking morrow,
 You moon-like lit the way I struggled o'er.

III.

Though as a cataract my soul went lashing
 Itself through ravines desolate and gray,
You made me see a beauty in the flashing,
 And with your presence diamonded the spray.

IV.

Then, Lenore, though we have grown much older—
 Though our eyes were brighter when we met,
Still let us feel, shoulder unto shoulder
 And heart to heart, above the world yet!

AT NIAGARA

THE RAPIDS.

I.

In broken lines, like ghosts of buried nations,
    Struggling beneath their white and tangled palls,
They leap and roar to Earth their exaltations,
    And Earth e'en trembles as each spectre falls.

II.

With strength that gives solemnity to clangour,
    With quaint immensity that strangles mirth,
Like mortal things they roar to time their anger,
    Like things immortal they disdain the Earth.

III.

They bound—as dallying in their gorgeous West,
    In forest cradles and in parent mountains,
They heard old Ocean throb his regal breast
    And call his vassals—the cascades and fountains.

IV.

From crag to crag they leap and spread the sound,
    Through gorge and wood their flashing banners motion,
Till here in frantic rivalry they bound,
    These mighty white-plumed cohorts, for the ocean.

V.

Surging along the pale battalions muster,
   Crowding each other, till the strongest springs
A-top his fellows, with heroic lustre,
   And dares the deeds, like Viking, that he sings.

VI.

Like men, the Rapids, born amid restless valor,
   Flash o'er their foes with many a frothened spasm,
And linking all in pomp's majestic pallor,
   Leap like ten thousand Romans down the chasm !

THE FALLS.

I.

There is an awful eloquence around—
   Like earthquake underneath the dreamful pillows
Of some great town, that deemed its strength profound
   And wakes on worse than frantic Ocean's billows.

II.

The mists, like shadowy cathedrals rise,
   And through the vapory cloisters prayers are pouring :
Such as ne'er sprang to the eternal skies,
   From old Earth's passionate and proud adoring.

III.

There is a voice of Scripture in the flood,
   With solemn monotone of glory bounding,

Making all else an awe-hushed solitude
　To hear its everlasting faith resounding.

IV.

There is a quiet on my heart like death,
　My eyes are gifted with a strange expansion,
As if they closed upon my life's last breath,
　And oped to measure the eternal mansion.

V.

I see so much I fear to trust my vision,
　I hear so much I doubt my mortal ear,
I feel so much, my soul in strong submission
　Bends in a silent, death-like rapture here.

SHANE'S HEAD.⁴

Scene—Before Dublin Castle. Night. A clansman of Shane O'Neill's discovers his chief's head upon a pole.

I.

God's wrath upon the Saxon! may they never know the
    pride,
Of dying on the battle-field, their broken spears beside ;
When victory gilds the gory shroud of every fallen brave,
Or death no tales of conquered clans can whisper to his
    grave.
May every light from Cross of Christ that saves the heart
    of man,
Be hid in clouds of blood before it reach the Saxon
    clan ;
For sure, O God !—and you know all whose thought for
    all sufficed,—
To expiate these Saxon sins, they'd want another Christ.

II.

Is it thus, O Shane the haughty ! Shane the valiant ! that
    we meet—
Have my eyes been lit by Heaven but to guide me to
    defeat ;
Have *I* no chief—or *you* no clan, to give us both de-
    fence,
Or must I, too, be statued here with thy cold eloquence ?

Thy ghastly head grins scorn upon old Dublin's Castle-
    tower,
Thy shaggy hair is wind-tost, and thy brow seems rough
    with power ;
Thy wrathful lips, like sentinels, by foulest treach'ry
    stung,
Look rage upon the world of wrong, but chain thy fiery
    tongue.

III.

That tongue whose Ulster accent woke the ghost of
    Columbkill,
Whose warrior words fenced round with spears the oaks
    of Derry Hill ;
Whose reckless tones gave life and death to vassals and
    to knaves,
And hunted hordes of Saxons into holy Irish graves.
The Scotch marauders whitened when his war-cry met
    their ears,
And the death-bird, like a vengeance, poised above his
    stormy cheers,
Ay, Shane, across the thundering sea, out-chanting it
    your tongue,
Flung wild un-Saxon war-whoopings the Saxon Court
    among.

IV.

Just think, O Shane ! the same moon shines on Liffey
    as on Foyle,
And lights the ruthless knaves on both, our kinsmen to
    despoil ;

6*

And you the hope, voice, battle-axe, the shield of us and
    ours,
A murdered, trunkless, blinding sight above these Dub-
    lin towers.
Thy face is paler than the moon, my heart is paler still—
My heart? I had no heart—'twas yours, *'twas* yours!
    to keep or kill.
And you kept it safe for Ireland, Chief,—your life, your
    soul, your pride,—
But they sought it in thy bosom, Shane—with proud
    O'Neill it died.

v.

You were turbulent and haughty, proud, and keen as
    Spanish steel,
But who had right of these, if not our Ulster's Chief—
    O'Neill?
Who reared aloft the "Bloody Hand" until it paled the
    sun,
And shed such glory on Tyrone, as chief had never done.
He was "turbulent" with traitors—he was "haughty"
    with the foe—
He was "cruel," say ye Saxons? Ay! he dealt ye blow
    for blow!
He was "rough" and "wild," and who's not wild, to see
    his hearthstone razed?
He was "merciless as fire"—ah, ye kindled him,—he
    blazed!
He was "proud:" yes, proud of birthright, and because
    he flung away
Your Saxon stars of princedom, as the rock does mock-
    ing spray.

He was wild, insane for vengeance,—ay ! and preached
  it till Tyrone
Was ruddy, ready, wild too, with " Red hands" to clutch
  their own.

VI.

" The Scots are on the border, Shane"—ye saints, he
  makes no breath—
I remember when that cry would wake him up almost
  from death :
Art truly dead and cold ? O Chief ! art thou to Ulster
  lost ?
" Dost hear, *dost hear ?* By Randolph led, the troops
  the Foyle have crossed !"
He's truly dead ! he must be dead ! nor is his ghost
  about—
And yet no tomb could hold his spirit tame to such a
  shout :
The pale face droopeth northward—ah ! his soul must
  loom up there,
By old Armagh, or Antrim's glynns, Lough Foyle, or
  Bann the Fair !
I'll speed me Ulster-wards, your ghost must wander there,
  proud Shane,
In search of some O'Neill, through whom to throb its
  hate again !

SAINT ANNE'S WELL.[1]

I.

ADOWN the loved valley of sweet Glan-nis-mole,
The Dodder's wild waters in bright rapture roll;
And woo the brown heath in its winding career,
Like a young lover stealthily pressing his dear:
Or yet, like the red Indian tracing the spot,
Where the white man has ravished his primeval cot;
And it steals and it foams, half in fear, half in joy,
Like a girl all beauty, all pride like a boy.
Looming over this valley, where Solitude reigns,
In all the wild stillness that Nature enchains,
Kippure has his throne,—where defying the gale,
Castle-Kelly enwraps with weird shadows the vale,—
His head in the clouds, as though bound with a crown,
His sceptre the rays of the sun streaming down,
His courtiers, Bal-mannoch, Cornaun, See-Finane,
From the Brakes to green Tallaght he boasts his domain:
And the Golden Spears, glistening like sentinels, stand
Near the throne of the chief of this bright valley-land
With his face to the Liffey, his back to Glancree,
Echo sings, as bard should, of his proud chieftaincy;
And the wind sweeping down—like the gray wizard
          powers
Of Homer, or Ossian, that Homer of ours—

Thrills the heather, like harp-strings, that vibrating loud,
Makes invisible chorus between cliff and cloud,
And hovers with many a mystical *rann*
O'er the fountain of goodness—the Well of St. Anne.

II.

The well calmly springs on the wild brocken side,
Like a tear on the cheek of a soul sanctified—
A sister of charity, given by bliss
To cure with its virtues, and cool with its kiss !
And dear is this valley !—ah, yes, ever dear
Are the scenes that are linked with a smile or a tear—
That thrilled us with pleasure, or filled us with pain,
In the noonday of life, and youth's royal domain !
What can be more dear than that one lonely place,
Where youth met its reflex in some young loved face ?
Saw the tremors, and wooings, the kissings, and then
Saw the quarrels and sobs, yea, and kissing again ;
Where the vale was our study—our music the brooks—
The graveyard our library—tombstones our books ;
And the Ruin, a monitor graybeard profound,
Full of pride in his charge of the records around.
And our Wells—holy Wells ! that our loved legends link—
Making sinew and soul of our past glory drink—
To the heroes that fought, and the lances that sprung
As the sage counselled battle, or poet war sung !
They are dear to our hearts : and remind dreaming man
Of the Action he's heir to !—loved Well of St. Anne.

III.

Its waters are clear, and as pure as the soul
Of the saint that endowed it.   Beneath a green knoll

It peacefully slumbers in hallowed repose,
And though always brimming, it never o'erflows;
For a sidelong trickle leads off the blest flow,
When its breast is too full, to the Dodder below;
And skirts by the little church Kilmosantan,
Where the green ivy close the old ruin doth span,
And clings like a lover, whose constancy wages
A war with old Time—growing fonder through ages !
On these lonely waters the saint left a spell,
Which faith have the people, and thence to the well
They fly for its draughts ; for the power Saint Anne
Bestowed on the spring was, that if mortal man
Was maimed, ill, but faith had, he'd surely get ease
If he creep from the church to the well on his knees.
Methinks few e'er try—for devious the path
To the sickling or sage; and the maimed one who hath
Strength eno' to proceed, needs less the spell, than
Stout patience he'd want to suit goodly Saint Anne.

IV.

Sweet Vale ! Holy Well ! shall this heart e'er forget,
This mind to thee die, or my sun of thought set
On the days I have lingered beside thy clear tide,
Or with those my heart clung to, clomb thy hill side ?
Pointing out the old raths, where the sage peasant told
Me, the fairies and spreethauns their wild revels hold ;
When I merrily laughed, and he solemnly chid,
Adjuring me gravely, to "mind what I did,"
Lest the "wee folk" in vengeance should give me a stroke.
Then I danced on the rath, half in doubt, half in joke,
And he, shaking his head, strolled away, chiding still,
And praying, " Heaven help my irreverent will."
Shall those scenes pass away, when afar I am gone ?

No! as steel to the magnet, I ever cling on!
No! my heart never shall let that picture decay;
Though I float the St. Lawrence, the famed thrush's lay
Of Glan-nis-mole's valley shall still charm mine ear,
And the wild Dodder's carol yet louder I'll hear
Than Niagara's chorus: the ivy's fresh love,
To my heart, as its temple, wherever I rove,
Will cling like a mantle to warm its veins,
With love for its youth's home, while feeling remains:
The church where I've dreamed all the summer days fair,
The cascades that burst like some wild Irish air—
Which flashing and fading, its force is scarce felt,
The passions so quick into low murmurs melt—
The furze-gilded uplands—the brier-bound brooks,
The moss-mottled crags, where the sun his last looks—
The Brakes, where the hills, shutting Wicklow out, stand,
Like the bulwarks and guards of some Bard's promised
    land—
And each hill, whose gray brow, bound with heath pur-
    ple-brown,
Seems a king with his iron but silken-cased crown—
Ah! where'er I may roam, these in fancy I'll scan,
And my mouth shall be still cool with draughts from
    Saint Anne.

WINTER THOUGHTS.

I.—THE DEAD YEAR.

I.

YET another chief is carried
   From life's battle on his spears,
To the great Valhalla cloisters
   Of the ever-living years.

II.

Yet another year—the mummy
   Of a warlike giant, vast—
Is niched within the pyramid
   Of the ever-growing past.

III.

Years roll through the palm of Ages,
   As the dropping ros'ry speeds
Through the cold and passive fingers
   Of a hermit at his beads.

IV.

One year falls and ends its penance,
   One arises with its needs,
And 'tis ever thus prays Nature,
   Only telling years for beads.

V.

Years, like acorns from the branches
    Of the giant oak of Time,
Fill the earth with healthy seedlings
    For a future more sublime.

II.—A FROSTY NIGHT.

I.

As one that worketh miracles, the moon
    Transfigures all the silence into light;
    And filagreed with frost the hill-sides white,
    And sloping uplands flecked with drifted snow,
    Seem, through their statued chill, to whine a low
And plaintive croon.

II.

The groves that were in summer-time all song,
    Profuse in clear soprano tones of glee,
    Now hoarsely dull, like voice-cracked choirs dree
    Their shivering existences, and make
    Night mournful, as the dirges slowly take
Their woes along.

III.

The mountain gorges, that like arteries ran
    With June-breath, hot as blood, are weirdly numb,
    And here and there the trickling streamlets come
    And break the frost in many a wild device,
    Struggling a-through thin barricades of ice
That all the gullies span.

7

IV.

The lonely trees, scant-robed in crispy snow,
    Stretching their bare arms upward to the sky,
    Seem like poor buried souls, who did not die,
    That waking, burst their sepulchres, and strive,
    With piteous plaints, to prove themselves alive
To their mad woe.

V.

As o'er the ghostly landscape peers the sight,
    The moonlight teaming an unbroken flood—
    The stars that in their planet coteries brood
    Over earth's solitude—the distant trackless sea—
    Roll to Thought's shore the ebbless tide—Eternity
This vast, pale night.

III.—SNOW ON THE GROUND.

I.

Like a corpse the stark earth lieth,
    Free from toiling Life's deceits ;
And the Air, grown pale from watching,
    Swathes her round with snowy sheets.

II.

Fold on fold wraps mutely round her,
    Her calm breast no life-hope rears,
And she seems from heaven's weeping,
    To be tombed in frozen tears.

III.

But though rigid cold her bosom,
 Gone her music—fled her bloom ;
Still the shrouded Earth, like Juliet,
 Is but tranced within the tomb.

IV.—SUMMER ALWAYS.

I.

WHILE the wind is fiercely howling,
 Lilla dear, come anear—
While the wolf-like wind is howling,
Round the cottage gables prowling,
And the wintry clouds are scowling
 On the mere :
Let us, waking up the embers,
 Love and youth and books revere,
Feel that howling bleak Decembers
 Cannot make a winter here,
  Lilla dear.

II.

While the outside world is shivering,
 Lilla dear, come anear—
While the beggar Earth is shivering,
Like a miser, old and quivering,
Unto Time his debt delivering
 Of the year :
Let us, clinging close together,
 Though perchance we drop a tear

O'er the past, find summer weather
　E'er in living, loving here,
　　Lilla dear.

———

V.—FACES IN THE FIRE.

I.

I am gazing all the night-time,
　At the faces in the fire—
Whilst the roaring rain-storm dashes
On the shaking window-sashes,
And the wakeful aerial ocean
Wracks the forest that it wrestles ;
And the sea, with wrathful motion,
Shakes and breaks the lab'ring vessels,
Till the crowded timbers, surging,
Send the people, wildly splurging,
　In the waves, till they expire.

II.

And I think how like the life-flame
　Are those red shapes I admire :—
First, they're merely indicated,
Then, like childhood, grow elated
With the fresh heat that imbues them,
Then like youth hot flames infuse them,
Then, like men, a steady burning
Glows a-through them, till the turning
Point of being, makes gray gashes,
And they crumble into ashes
　Like mere faces in the fire.

WASHINGTON.[1]

I.

ART in its mighty privilege receives
  Painter and painted in its bonds forever ;
A girl by Raphael in his glory lives—
A Washington unto his limner gives
  The Ages' love to crown his best endeavor

II.

The German Emperor, with whose counterpart
  The gorgeous Titian made the world acquainted,
Boasted himself immortal by the art ;
But he who on *thy* features cast his heart,
  Was made immortal by the head he painted !

III.

For thou before whose tinted shade I bow,
  Wert sent to show the wise of every nation
How a young world might leave the axe and plough
To die for Truth ! So great, so loved wert thou,
  That he who touched thee won a reputation.

IV.

The steady fire that battled in thy breast,
  Lit up our gloom with radiance, good though gory ;

7*

Like some red sun which the dull earth caressed
Into a wealthy adoration blest
   To be its glory's great reflected glory.

v.

Thou—when the earthly heaven of man's soul—
   The heaven of home, of liberty, of honor—
Shuddered with darkness—didst the clouds uproll
And burst such light upon the nation's dole
   That every State still feels thy breath upon her.

vi.

Could I have seen thee in the Council—bland,
   Firm as a rock, but as deep stream thy manner;
Or when, at trembling Liberty's command,
Facing grim havoc like a flag-staff stand,
   And squadrons rolling round thee like a banner!

vii.

Could I have been with thee on Princeton's morn!
   Or swelled with silence in the midnight muster;
Beheld thee ever, every fate adorn—
Or on retreat, or wingèd victory borne—
   The warrior throbbing with the sage's lustre:

viii.

Could I have shouted in the wild acclaim
   That rent the sky o'er Germantown asunder;
Or when, like cataract, 'gainst the sheeted flame
You dashed, and chill'd the victor-shout to shame,
   On Monmouth's day of palsy-giving thunder:

IX.

Could I have followed thee through town and camp!
    Fought where you led, and heard the same drums rattle :
Charged with a wild but passion-steadied tramp,
And witnessed, rising o'er death's ghastly damp,
    The stars of empire through the clouds of battle!

X.

Oh! to have died thus 'neath thy hero gaze,
    And won a smile, my bursting youth would rather
Than to have lived with every other praise,
Saving the blessing of those epic days
    When you blest all, and were the nation's father.

XI.

The autumn sun caresses Vernon's tomb,
    Whose presence doth the country's honor leaven :
Two suns they are, that dissipate man's gloom ;
For one's the index to Earth's free-born bloom,
    The other to our burning hope in Heaven!

XII.

Thy dust may moulder in the hollow rock ;
    But every day thy soul makes some new capture!
Nations unborn will swell thy thankful flock,
And Fancy tremble that she cannot mock
    Thy history's Truth that will enchant with rapture.

XIII.

How vain the daring to compute in words
    The height of homage that the heart would render!
And yet how proud—to feel no speech affords
Harmonious measure to the subtle chords
    That fill the soul beneath thy placid splendor!

THE PLAINT OF THE WILD-FLOWER.

I.

I was not born for the town,
Where all that's pure and humble's trodden down :
My home is in the woods—
The over-arching, cloistered solitudes ;
Where the full-toned psalm
Of Nature at her matin broke the calm
Of cloudy pillowed Night,
With calmness made more voluble by light :
And where the Minstrel Noon,
Made every young stem spring, as to a tune ;
Ay, where our joys were led
To suit the fluted measures of the orb o'erhead.
I am forlorn
Here 'mid the waking jargon of the day ;
Noon brings no light, no song of birds at play ;
My plume is in the dust : I pine and pray
For the old woods, the grand old woods away
Where I was born.

II.

Here I am dying : I want room—
Room for the air of heaven, for the bloom

Of never-tiring nature ; room
For the verdure-freighted clouds, and thunder-boom
    That sounds relief to drouthy earth ;
Room for the sunlight and th' exhaustless mirth
    Of laughing July's breeze,
Untangling the meshes of the branching trees ;
    Room for cool night and ruddy day,
For peace, for health—aught naturally gay ;
    Room to take vital breath
And look on any thing not painted death !
    I am forlorn—
I, who from my earliest golden age,
Sat by the regal Oak's foot, like a page,
And, mantled in moss, at the close of day
Slept by my prince, in the woods far away
    Where I was born.

III.

    Here is no room—no room
For e'en a flower's life ; nothing but a tomb.
    O forest gods ! look down,
And shield your other offspring from the town.
    Ah ! would that I could die
Where o'er my wreck the forest flowers might sigh,
    And clustering shrubs a-near
Weave dirges low, like leaves above my bier ;
    Where kindly chestnut-leaves
Would shade the woe of every plant that grieves,
    And e'en the great Oak's head
Let fall the tears of dew when his poor page is dead
    I am forlorn :
Night brings no darkness, and the day no light ;

Noon brings but noise, to vary my affright;
I'm dying 'neath the city's loathsome blight,
Far, O my mother Nature! from thy sight,
Far from *thy* earth, *thy* heaven, and the woodland
         bright
     Where I was born.

GAME LAWS.[1]

I.

A-THROUGH the crunching underwood the wild boar madly
    came,
With lashing tail and gleaming tusks, stiff mane and eyes
    of flame.

II.

Through golden crops, through tangled copse, he fiercely
    plunging tore,
All seemed but withered fibres to the rage-expanding
    boar.

III.

Through leafy screen and rough ravine, through lane and
    plain the brute
Makes head, and in the cotter's field at last eludes
    pursuit.

IV.

" Ho ! Hans, be quick ; take in the child—bring out my
    trusty gun."
Hans fled and came, the cotter fired—the wild boar's
    race was run.

V.

But woe ! alas, what came to pass, the forest-ranger saw
The deed, and shot the cotter down—to make him " keep
    the law."

VI.

Herr Graff and staff, feast, laugh, and quaff that night
    with beakers red :
The cotter's home is desolate—its head, its heart lies
    dead.

VII.

'Tis royal sport for king and court to hunt the grizzly
    boar,
But woe unto the poor man who dares hunt him from
    his door.

DREAMING BY MOONLIGHT.

Scene—*A Public Park in the City.*
Persons—*Two Students.*

PICTOR.

Look at the pale Moon pacing up the skies,
Like a frayed maiden who had seen her sire,
The martial Sun, the monarch of the day,
Hunted before the red and spearlike clouds,
Whose only glory is the blood he shed :
See her, all pale and beautifully wan,
O'erlooking where her overpowered sire,
Ennobling the foes he crimsoned with his gore,
Sank ; but, in sinking, died the victor's death,
And dragged them with him from all earthly gaze.

LEON.

She looks divine !

PICTOR.

She *is* divine ! . . . . . but see how white she grows,
As though her regnant spirit was congeal'd
With thinking on her sire's red sacrifice—
Or though the horror of the mighty death
Frightened away her outraged blood, and sent
Her woman's milken feeling through her frame ;

8

As on she hurries panting from the East—
And up th' uncertain blue with steady pace,
Made regular in weakness, she persists—
To preach her vengeance to the starry hosts,
And try to win them to her filial cause.

LEON.

Oh ! would we could her frenzied pleading hear—
For see, yon stars seem gaining greater light
From the infusion of her earnest speech ;
She stirs their souls ; they glimmer with her thought,
And nod, as to each other, their applause !
Oh ! how her orphaned virginhood must rise
Into the woman's proud, full-statured force,
Making her importunities, commands !—
How she must picture the old hero's death,
And make the roused heavens think he lives again,
Pleading his own cause with accustomed fire !
She grows with her desire—expands in agony,
And reaches with her light the furthest star.

PICTOR.

But they are motionless—they seem so rapt
With her enthusiasm, they bestir them not ;
Her eloquence has fixed them where they stand.

LEON.

Ay doth she kill the cause by the effect
She makes. Her bright, divine intelligence
Run loose upon the sky—the stars are vague
To aught but listening : *I* blame them not,

For who could stir while yet her voice enchants,
And flings its spells of eloquence around.

PICTOR.

Would I were Venus, and I'd win them all,
As she did Paris, to my suit; I'd make
Their test of vassalage and price of court
An unconditioned service to the Moon.
I would, by all the beauty of her crest!
I would, or if they lacked the val'rous soul,
Or paced in stolid ease while yet she prayed
I'd change them, as the Cyprian fair she did,
To moody oxen, and confer them horns
Less hard than their own hearts.—But look!

LEON.

Mars reddens: like a man, his face suffused
With all the gory passion of his heart
That prompts his brain to bloodier deeds
Than crimsoning his own cheeks: yet see the Moon
Untired, with luminous distention praying
Aid from the trancèd orbs—wasting her soul
Upon the statued crowd, who give no sign
They hearken to her speech, save that their fronts
Beam in the light her radiant sorrow sheds,
Would I were Mars! O Pictor! would I were,
And by the heavens I'd hold in my own right,
I'd leap from out my hero couch of clouds,
And marshalling the Scythian hordes in air,
I'd drive these laggard constellations hence,
And pale them in the visage of the Sun
Avenged!   (*Muses for a few moments.*)

A hero's *name* can conquer worlds ;
The action dies not, though the body rots :
And I would shout " The Sun" through every space
Till all the echoes wrangled into *one*—
Like foes towards a well-fought battle's close.
Then like a Joshua I'd command it—stand—
Making that day eternity in Heaven !
So that these stars might have devouring rest
As stagnant waters grow beneath the Sun
To eat themselves up with the things they breed.
Ah ! yonder stars—these ancient godships feel
Their former deeds ill-qualify the seats
They now usurp throughout the modern Heaven,
And fear to move, lest moving they're unthroned ;
As though the sitting on a throne made kings
Or gods, or transfused souls in slimy men.
A king is he whose regnant soul acts king !
Men can be gods 'mong men who act the god,
And every dastard is himself the mark
Showing how far below his knavish heart
The tide of virtue flings the weeds of vice.
Look at the Moon, so passionately pure—
See how she knocks unpitied at their hearts,
Like outcast Virtue at a city's gates
Where " merchant princes" star commercial skies.
And now—expanding in her strength of woe,
She rises o'er the senseless myriads there
To shield her virgin pride from heartless gaze.
See—with eyes turned for comfort to her heart,
As plant that closes to the vulgar touch,
And pale determination on her brow,
And sobs unuttered, making her bare breast
In expectation rigid, as they wait

Upon her mouth, as prisoner upon
The gates, to heave his presence to the air—
She paces queenlike to yon murky cloud,
And seeks a refuge in the weighty gloom:
As virgin martyrs her god-ripened years
In solemn, solitary, cloister dim,
Seeking within the empire of her faith
Amends for that cold, senseless world she fled—
And lo ! the people who had passed her by,
Or gazed at her for beauty's sake alone,
Proclaim in gossip all the worth gone with her.
So, all the stars seem whispering of the Moon ;
They actually brighten, as inspired,
Now she is gone, in pity for her fate.
Poor Moon—thou art the type of intellect,
And all mankind but imitate the stars.

PICTOR.

'Tis true—too true : but, Leon, let us on.
Like Rembrandt's shadows is the atmosphere,
Darkly and deeply clear, to night.

LEON.

Ay, good !
And through it brood yon clouds, as ponderous as
The prophet brow of Angelo's Isaiah.

PICTOR.

Leon, let us on—the air refreshes like a bath :
It turns quaint fancies in my dreaming brain,
Like a Kaleidoscope : all the shiftless thoughts,
On which the humid noon lay like muffed glass,

8*

Now deftly turn, and tumble into pictures.
This night air's like iced wine, it cools the brain
And warms the fancy.   Bah, these August days,
When the red noon like a huge blanket folds
The summer, hushing up the city's energy
Into a sluggish, dreamless heat, are horrible—
I can only breathe o'nights.

LEON.

The day's hot jargon, with its clamors rude,
Clangs on my ear as doth the discord mean
When miser huckster rings a poor man's coin.
It speaks of traffic, doubts, and selfish ends;
The whole sensation of the day is Cash.
You can't enjoy it save you quit the town;
And seek sweet nature on the broad highways;
In crooked lanes where vine-clad banks are fanned,
By lithe witch-hazel and young maple boughs;
In yellow woods with nuts incrusted o'er;
Or, by the margins of the elfin streams,
That dance in white-capped groups a-through the
        rocks,
And then join hands to rush o'er level sands.
You leave the city to enjoy the day:
But in this park, within the city's heart,
With fabrics dim, like battlements around,
We can enjoy the calm and placid night.
Night speaks a language known to every tongue;
When I unfold my heart to her, I feel
As though I spoke to every troubled soul.
Her starry syllables each land translates
Into the universal blessing—rest.
In every clime the lover trusts in her;

From her the sorrow-laden find response :
She is munificence itself to grief.
On her pale breast the wretched outlaw rests ;
The beggar views the starlight as a king,
Yea, like a monarch he in moonlight walks,
When day, like monarch, walks upon his rags.
And to the student's vague and longing breast
Is not the vast impenetrable night
A fit companion?   And to those
Thrice happy hearts, who at the Throne of thrones,
Seek upon bended knee sweet recompense,
And all-supplying dues for the defaults
Of life, what time so prayerful as night
To make their peace with Heaven ere they sink
Into that temporary death called sleep.

PICTOR.

Truly thou art enraptured with the night,
And break thy fantasies upon her grace,
As lovers do upon their first love's love.
Think her thy mistress, and but woo her thus,
She'll doubtless graft upon thy ardent brain
The various benefits you crown her with.

LEON.

The Moon-souled midnight is the Poet's love,
Pale with reflection of the sunny world
Of books and thought : her placid forehead bound
With strands of lustrous stars, but brilliant less
Than all the teeming radiances within.
Her wavy locks in pale effulgence hang
Around them with prophetic dreaminess,

As doth the Revelations of Saint John,
Around the light on his enthusiast brain.
Her eyes are blue, as blue as Huron's lake ;
And like it clear, in which the gazer sees,
Through magic vistas of refracted light,
Her pure soul bathing in their azure depths
And flinging gems out as a nymph from cave.
As Huron's lake her eyes ; their lashes dark
Like the tall fir-trees, black against the sky,
Which are reflected in the moon-lit lake,
And let the light flood through their lashy web
As water teems out from a fisher's net,
And leaves the silver-fish within it caught,
Yet leaping brilliance in the silken jail.

PICTOR.

Bravo !   Perchance in presence of the fair
You have described, you would outline the bard,
Who hath so great a passion for her !

LEON.

You can no more describe the Poet, than
You can make rules to judge of poetry.

PICTOR.

Yet critics have at both ! why not ?

LEON.

                 Because
True poetry, is truthful thought made plain ;
Deep love of Nature, Man, and God ! that brings
To each heart's empire, humbly, howsoe'er,

The greatest good, and lifts its feelings up
To man and God with pure dependent faith!
Can we make rules to measure each heart's need?
Only the Poet in his prophet vein
Comes near that power.

PICTOR.

Yet we have rules—

LEON.

True, which but prove they're useless to true song.
Whence come these rules by captious critics made?
From great bard's works to frighten lesser ones.
All poets are not Shaksperes, yet they're judged
By rules which Shakspere's excellence suggests.
One might as well o'errule the tender stars
Because they're not like the creating sun.
You would not crush th' aspiring creeping rose,
Because it cannot be a centuried oak!

PICTOR.

No, truly; 'twere too bad our sweethearts wore
Nor rose nor violet on their breast or hair
Because forsooth the oak's thy king of plants.

LEON.

No.   Let the blessèd ones be decked with flowers!
Those blooming gems were sent for woman's care.
They are the fragrant wealth of innocence—
The silent courtiers that in gardens bow
In thankful blossoms to the gentle queens

By whose sweet leave and favor they are there.
Oh, bless the girls! especially bless those
Who honor Nature in the love of flowers.
So should we have a blessing for the bard
Who, though he grasps not the quick changing hues
Of life's great scenes, in all their epic shifts,
Cultures the flowers and harmonies of life :
His heart is right.

PICTOR.

        We cannot give too much
Of honest recompense to those who live
Alone to tend the beautiful.

LEON.

            Recompense ?
How can you recompense the Poet's heart,
Which hath more wealth than lurid placers yield ?
The Poet's heart encompasses the world, .
And throbs great futures into fancied life.
He knows all past, and as a cloud o'er moon
Passes the present, stealing all its light,
And floats up farther heavens unknown to us
Where other moons make night to other worlds,
And other suns, like fiery burnished bits,
Rein in their charging satellites as steeds.
He thinks vast futures, which, if born aright,
Shall hold his image as the son his sire's.
He flies through futures as a seed through storm,
That falls to rise a cedar.   Ay, he hews
Out from that mine of mist, to-morrow,
Deep echoing temples for his soul's repose,

And dwells in them to-day :—as Shakspere loosed
The gusty currents of his Boreal soul
Through the tone-fashioning valleys of his brain,
Which sprang such sounds two centuries ago
As have not ended yet ; so that no ear
Can know the echo from the voice itself.
Where shall its gathering echoes end ?   Oh where !
If 'twill not live this third-rate world out,
This minor fragment of the Godhead's work,
And float it full of song and sense along
The turbulent and greedy sea of Time,
Dash it to chaos as a sacrifice,
And harmonize the crash of crumbling worlds !

                                   [*A pause.*

The Poet's recompense is in being a Poet !
The most Earth can do is not let him starve.

PICTOR.

I pray you, Leon, let's not talk o' that,
The Beautiful will drive us into earth,
Like moles, if she but hear us mutter " bread."
Come, let us feed upon the stars.

LEON.

            Heavenly night !
Night such as this is truly Poet's food.

PICTOR.

And Painter's also my exclusive friend.

LEON.

And are not Painters Poets with the brush ?
It is their Prospero-wand—it is the rod

By which, as Franklin drew the heavenly fire,
They draw all nature's brilliance to their will!
The canvas is his world, o'er which supreme,
The artist looks creation like a god,
Seeing vast nature's there while yet 'tis blank.
He smiles, 'tis peopled; mountains lap the skies,
Thick plaided woods hang robe-like round their loins;
Rivers leap forth with glad primeval chants;
Streamlets run babbling, laughing in his face,
Like little children who *may* smile at God;—
Valleys yawn open at his peaceful nod;
Oceans are raging when he thinks in thunder;
Ships riven sink beneath his light'ning eye;
Flowers chant perfume to his summer thought;
And he surrounds all, as the air his earth!
Is not this poetry?   The very thought
Matins my own aspiring dawn for verse,
And drags up all my wild desires and love,
Like ghosts from out the sultry tomb of noon,
Where they were sepultured, not dead, but tranced
Thine is a marvellous art, my friend,
And thou hast genius, too—genius, like a sun,
To richen your ambition, send a pulse,
And life, and bright transfusion into all
It smiles upon: but you must labor, too,
Like that great orb, and heat the canvas into action
So that when you, with honor doubled, sink,
Your locks grown golden, as in infant age,
With all the sun-tinct trophies of your art,
Your every picture, like a starry world,
Shall hold a fixed, mysterious wealth to earth,
And, all combined, be galaxy of stars—
An orbed and systemed heaven in which, unseen

Saving through them, as their creator, you
Shall look and live eternal !

PICTOR.

Fling not, Leon, the lasso of thy tongue
So wildly around my brain : you make me mad,
And only weaken me with passion, dumb.
The golden net you weave around my heart
Is blood-stained, as it swells to its capacity
And bursts.   I plunge in your great fantasy,
Like a man at sea, mocked at each plunge,
Yet plunging still to overleap the waves,
Those liquid gods, that, white-lipped, sneer me down.
As well might valley-huddled stream leap up
And kiss the hill-tops, which alone kiss heaven,
As I attempt the laurel that you shake :
You place the destiny too infinite,
The crown too high.

> [*The Students walk on in silence.   After a
> long pause, and suddenly,* PICTOR *resumes,
> musingly :*]

Yet I have been no orphan to such thoughts,
But they were in less vivid frenzies draped.
[*Enthusiastically.*]   Ay, I have oft before my
     easel stood
Watching my soul take shapes o' the canvas—
Flinging my color-laden palette there,
As Jove cast Saturn's blood into the sea,
And saw it rise a goddess !   I have stood
Facing this new heaven like a continent,
And felt my ambitious thoughts, like rivers,
Glut the deep secret ravines of my heart,
Cataract over obstacles, and spread

On, growing stronger for an ocean bound ;
That ocean, like *all* seas, immortal !   [*A pause*
Are we not equal to our dreams ?

LEON.

We are.
The dreams of poets are their lives' programmes.
Even their *acts* are dreams to lesser men,
And they themselves alone can act their dreams.
Dreams to such men are beacons where to go ;
They rest the body, but ne'er calm the brain ;
And while flesh sleeps the soul allots its work.
When eyelids kiss eyelids, like a fondling pair,
And say " Good-night" before they lock in sleep,
Then to the outward world the poet rests ;
The while his body, like a listless cloud
Scarce motioning in summer noon, is free,
And warmed to quiet by his soul's loud songs,
As is the cloud by sunlight.
A brilliant future is before you friend :
As lantern looks right on the shadows down ;
Fling out your soul, and make your own path clear.

PICTOR.

If I could undream all my dreams in acts,
Baptize in colors all my waking thoughts,
Drag them like culprits to the face of day,
And sentence them to service, I might be,
As oft I vainly hoped, a people's love,
The worshipped of a race ! the painter, who
Shed lustrous tribute greater far than gold
Upon the State I dwelt in, and was reared,

As on a monument of human hearts,
Above the taxes of official seal,
As Titian was in Venice !⁹   A wise
And most uncommon prince was Charles the Fifth,
Who boasted triple immortality.

LEON.

Ha ! monarchs not seldom lie !

PICTOR.

But he spoke truth,
For Titiano painted him three times.

LEON.

By all the gods, such glory makes one shake,
As though the gray, rapt antiquaries were
Fing'ring one's skeleton, and muttering
Low in reverence—" these are Pictor's bones,
The wondrous Artist he, and *these* Leon's
The Poet."   If we are sepultured a-close
I'll nudge thee then—you laugh, but I'm for fame ;
For I shall link my verses with your works,
Ay, like name upon your tomb, to *live* there,
And become immortal ; coaxing the ages'
Praise, for that like them, I knew you famous.
As Giovanni Strozzi for all time
Stands on an epigram, he wrote on him
The Arts' Arch-angel Michael, Angelo !

PICTOR.

Your sarcasm is winning in its fancy
And only proves how prone you poets are

To make mankind your debtors.　Yet Leon
In rich Johannisberg I'd drink to you
And your imagination, if I could.

LEON.

Bah! rich wine makes not honest wishes riche,
It only floats the loose straws of the wits
Iuto a bundle on the praise-choked ear.

PICTOR.

Well, here's may you as great a Poet be,
As you would fain so make an Artist me!

LEON.

So you fling back my measure of *your* worth
On me as the daguerreotypist does—
A likeness only without natural hues.
Ah!　Flattery—thou'rt used to coloring;
I need it not as most your sitters do,
For I have wed my heart unto my brain.
My heart, like woman, full of pure desires
Warms the wild current of her husband's will,
And by uniting with his purpose, hers,
Keeps all his forces disciplined by love:
So they are *one*, reliant, strong, and pure.
As two young streams that fled their parent hills,
Conscious of beauty, reckless in their strength,
Ambitioning to travel through an earth,
Are madly bounding to'ards a chasm unseen.
Haply they meet, and gallant by the way,
Soon they expand, like lovers' thought, and kiss
In one foam-passionate, convincing love ;

And clinging closer in the shadowy gorge,—
As wife and husband in misfortune's gloom,—
In one great span,—as rainbow in the skies
Aug'ring of good, or sunbeams o'er the cloud
Leap to the earth,—they near the brink, and *then*,
In one wild throb—love's sacrificial spasm,
They clear the rock, fling off their doubt in mist,
Heave in joy's agony at the danger past,
And, more than ever in each other twined,
Pace broadly onward through a wondering world.

PICTOR.

'Tis a bold metaphor, and an apt,
According well with your fine, frenzied,
Rapturous decision.

LEON.

       As those wed streams,
So of my heart and brain. Wild, riotous,
Unknown to each, as stars of various men
After rough speculation they have met,
Thank Heaven, not too late, and shudder o'er
The whispered stories of their reckless past.
My head and heart, like Moses' arms, are up
For victory! Goliath-browed Despair,
That giant evil falls,—my will the David!
You need not stare—I am not crazed, but love,
Passionately love the beautiful!
The wise, the great, the pure, soul-worthy great;
The trees, the rocks, the rivers, and the wind;
Earth, all its prized and unknown places; ay,
For here I learn, what no man knew before,
The heavens and all its vast localities

Of stars, I love with trembling vibrant soul,
In one heart-easing word—love GOD.

> *[A silence of some time: Leon resumes*
> *with enthusiastic calmness.*

Pictor, what I aspire to, I will be,
Or swallow up myself, as the ocean
Swallows the rain it once sent to the skies.

PICTOR.

With such a courage you deserve to win;
'Tis honor, friend, with courage such to fail;
I have the heart, but not the head to win,
While you seem born to fill up some great space:
Your brain is like a ball of silken thread,
Which may be woven into vast extent
As great in texture as in lustre rare.

LEON.

The Campanero in the southern woods,
With its white-bosomed, resonant appeal,
Makes all the silence-shrouded forest-trees
Start from their rest, for many miles around,
As convent-bell its votaries to prayer.
So when I sing, all distance shall be near,
In the wide universal echo.
I'll break upon men's reveries my song,
As Campanero on the dreaming leaves;
Or, like the Tinamou, that lonely bird,[10]
I'll utter one shrill cry—and men shall drop
The axe, or stay their rumbling teams—
Maids shall lean closer to the swarthy arms
And bend their heads to hear whence comes that
       sound

Half melancholy, half defiant shriek,
Which they shall never hear again.
I shall sing loud at intervals, or but once,
And then no more. I quail not to go on;
My only fear is to recede in thought.
Behind me, like a ship, there is a billowy surge,
Before, expansive wastes to be ploughed up;
Prophetic Heaven, as one vast choir, sings "go on,"
And earthly nature in its fruits and flowers
Like chanting acolytes respond.
Why, when I lift my forehead to the Sun
Does he not make my onward pathway clear,
And that I've trod gloom with my own shadow.

                        [*Clock strikes.*

PICTOR.

One—two—three—four—ah! bless me, it is dawn!
How fast the hours speed in talking.—
Four o'clock—let us for home: but where's the
       Moon?
Oh! see how haggard and out-tired she looks,
As lonely now she wanders broken-souled,
Scarcely the shadow of her beauteous self.
And all the stars are well-nigh fled away,
To dream of her unhappiness and fate;
Save here and there, some tender-hearted one,
Lingers who is not resolute to go
His way, or either follow her with cheer.
Mayhap the dead fire of her eloquence
Still spurts in embers on his soul's chilled hearth—
Who pales in sorrow for his acts to her,
And riven in consternation for her fate,
Sinks purposeless in silence where he stands.

LEON.

So men who're cowards and of bloodless hearts,
Or cold and stagnant ones, but brains enough
In silent flights, to dare a future think,
Yet lack the courage to construct upon
The certain present coming ages claim.
The fools know not that those who live when dead,
Are never dead when living.

              Here, Pictor,
Here is a picture for your brush,—see where,
Just over the horizon, undulate
Those pale, flushed clouds, as though the yestreen's
      Sun,
That sank, like dying hero, in his gore—
Was stirring in the shroud that swathed him round,
And sent his luminous action through the folds,
As though he felt he was *not* dead, but slept,
And struggled through his cerements to prove
The conscious glory to the weeping earth.
See too, like her whose son the Saviour raised,
The mute, dun Heaven, like a widow stands—
An awed-hope slightly ruddying her weeds,
Her ashen pallor daring not to flee,
Until she sees—oh mystery!—her son
Unshrouded, living, breathing, panting, move
Up from the couch, she dreamt alone, of death.

PICTOR.

Now may the heartless planets tremble ever,
And wailing Moon rejoice.

LEON.

            But no—she flies
Frightened unto death's shadowy texture,

Stricken in the presence of the rising Sun.
Her woman's terror giving fright full speed,
She vanishes before what seems to her
The gory spirit of her murdered sire.
And on through vast eternities she runs,
Distracted, plaining, superstitious, frayed ;
Loving the night, as sorrow loves the gloom,
For then her heart may gush a daughter's love
In orphaned abnegation of all bliss ;
Save of her stately purity thus loving.
Weak with her wail, distraught with fancies wild,
Haunted with loving memories, she beholds
Her glorious sire's lurid ghost appear
With every dawn, and barely able, flies ;
While he hot-hearted, not less loving, lights
The heavens all day to tell her, he is there.

So the eternal chase goes ever on ;
The Sun, like reason, with his broadcast light
Rising forever to explain the doubts,
The fear-suggested nothings of the dark,
The mist-made mountains, sombre shadowed groups
And filmy pageants of the moon-struck hours.
While she, the Moon, pale superstition's queen,
The monarch of the realms of fay
And elf and goblin, witch and boneless ghost ;
Reflections of her wail, as she of Sun,
For fanatics e'er throng gaunt Reason's wake
Until he, goaded with their insane shouts,
Turns on the mob with bright, determined eyes ;
And disconnects them in the face of day,
And wakeful men, from Truth's unhowled calm
    Faith :—

Ay she, the Moon, pale superstition's queen,
The prophetess of most devoted slaves,
Loud Ignorance and tongueless Fear, dreads Light,
For which grave Error ever says she seeks.
Most doubting men fear most to be convinced,
Yet preach most piously they thirst for fact.
The moon-brained on their own diseases feed :
And some who, sunless in a dungeon's vault,
Have lived like moles,—die when they see the light.
And then for some, black error hath such bliss,
From long experience, that a virtuous life
Brings them a solitude—a quiet hell,
A spirit-maddening calm, like calm at sea
To storm-tost craft, whose hold but echoes hath.
So of the frayed Moon, and the rising Sun.
Thus the eternal chase goes ever on,
Chill Superstition wailing through the gloom,
Till Nature, flattered that she pains for truth,
Sends up refulgent Reason on her path ;
But Superstition, knowing not the day,
Affrighted, flies off at the name of Light.

EFFIE GRAY.

WE may watch, and we may wait—
  Hope, till hoping bringeth pain,
But she ne'er will pass the gate—
  Effie cannot come again.

She was like some flower of Spring,
  Seeking Summer but to die,
When the very graves can bring
  Beauty to the heart and eye;
When each mound, like throbbing breast,
  Seems to heave with less of pain
Than of conscious pleasure, pressed
  By June's loving arms and brain:
    Arms that press with soothing sway,
    Brain enwreathed with flowers,
These are meet for the night that ne'er finds day—
  Meet for the rest of Effie Gray,
    Though fraught with gloom for ours.

We may dream she's coming soon,
  But we dupe our hopes in vain:
She is off—the Bride of June!
  Effie will not come again.

She is gone with the lordly June
  Of the fragrant blood and brow,
And the flowers croon a bridal tune,
  Though to us 'tis a death-chant now.
Oh ! her face was bright as morn,
  And her eyes were dark as night,
And her lips had a sunny scorn,
  Defending the weak or the right ;
And her locks, like the loosened tresses
  On some ripe Bacchante's head,
Wove sibylline caresses
  Round the eyes that thither sped !
    Fit Queen, I ween, for June the proud
    With his leaf-woven caves and bowers—
Though her laugh be hushed, and her robe a shroud,
  Take pride in thy bride, O June, the proud,
    She is fairest among thy flowers.

Hope we may, if hope we must,
  To allay our brooding pain ;
But the hinge be rust, and the gate be dust,
  Ere fair Effie comes again.

She passed through this tearful earth,
  Like a sun-ray through the rain,
Making diamonds in the dearth,
  With her woman's heart and brain.
For her heart was like the shower
  In July with bliss replete ;
And her brain, the mystic power
  Of the Indian Summer's heat.
Oh ! of rich and sparkling vintage
  Was her nature bubbling up,

Till Death, the reckless drunkard,
  Drank the draught, and crushed the cup.
    No human hand may deck the grave
    Of Effie Gray with flowers ;
For the sun through the noon, and at night the moon
  Whispers life into many a rare festoon,
    As never might spring from hand like ours.

THE PARTING OF THE SUN.

I.

IT was evening by the Hudson, and the Sun in conscience
    blest
With all the joy he gave that day, went nobly down to rest ;
Like some great benefactor, gliding off with happy mien,
O'erjoyèd with his power to bless, yet blushing because
    seen.

II.

Yet he lingered for a moment, as to crown his silent mirth,
By witnessing in one last glance, the comfort he gave
    Earth,
And seemed to say, " God bless you," while all nature
    unto him
Sent back the prayer a thousand-fold from stream and
    leafy limb.

III.

The humble shrub that hugged the Earth doth homage
    humbly bring—

Like all good loving offspring who around their mother
    cling,
And repaying back her kindness, flower a-near the aged
    sod—
And thrill with low-born eloquence of thanks to Nature's
    God.

IV.

Like other earthly children who have mental strength
    and growth,
The Poet Oak, the Elm Sage, and thoughtful Willow,
    loth
To cramp the rich exuberances that throb their pulses,
    dare
Possess the mist like minstrels and make music with the
    air.

V.

And the Kaatskills, bleak as sorrow, with their gray heads
    to the sky,
Seemèd mute in contemplation, loth to bid the Sun good-
    by :
With their broad backs turned westward, as though grief
    would not allow
Them face their friend, and feel his smile grow weak
    upon their brow.

VI.

They fain would live in memories of the noon, like sage
    who cheers
In gossiping of long lost joys that sunned his manhood's
    years—

But the anxious mist, like gathering tears, creep deftly
    o'er their breast,
And circling thence, like blood, rush up the sorrow to
    their crest.

VII.

And the Hudson, like a courier, doth with serious fury
    run,
To bear old hoary Ocean the last message of the Sun ;
Where the Congress of the river-gods in coral halls hold
    feast,
And bid the waves go welcome in his dawning in the
    East.

VIII.

And the tall trees weep in shadows, for happily know
    they
The Sun can't see the gloom he casts around when forced
    away,
And kindly show their brightest sides to soothe the part-
    ing pain,
While Day and Night's weird offspring, Eve, speeds up the
    eastern plain.

. . . .

IX.

There's a silence, like that moment when the drear fact
    feeds the blast,
That the golden sands of some great god of earth have
    run their last,
And noiseless round his couch the world, the nurse, Night,
    one by one,
Drapes the dun curtains of the clouds, and mutters pale—
    " He's gone."

HE WRITES FOR BREAD.

I.

Time—'tis midnight : Scene—a Garret:
Dramatis Personœ—two :
One, with wintry locks of silver—
    One, with locks of dark-brown hue.
And the old man sits him calmly,
    Speaking nothing, while his face,
With its quiet depth of meekness,
    Sheds a radiance on the place.
But, God! could we unfold his soul,
    And read the epic there,
We would not wonder at his thought,
    Nor whiteness of his hair.
Anon, he strangles to a sigh,
    Some heart-ache upward led ;
            Lest by a word
            He'd break the chord
    Of song that's wildly flitting
    Through the brain of him that's sitting,
Gushing out his very heart's blood
    On the page before him spread—
For through the night the young man kneads
    His brain for their daily bread.

II.

See, his pen toils slower, slower ;
 Now he talks his dreams aloud ;
And—he hastes to wrap his fancy
 In the pale expectant shroud :
For every sheet his brain-thoughts fill,
 Each line his keen wants crave,
But wrap and bind by piecemeal down
 The youth to an early grave.
Those little characters he inks,
 Are all grim Death's abetters ;
He does not nobly die at once,
 But sinks to his grave by letters.
And now his jaded thought would lag
 To soothe his aching head ;
   But he cannot wait,
   For the empty plate
   Reflects back his stare
   For the loaf *not* there :
But the old man *is* there—O God ! must he starve
While legions of other men's fathers are fed ?
The pang's inspiration ! The madhouse and love
 Are gambling for him who is writing for bread.

III.

He writes to make the readers laugh,
 When his heart's full with tears,
And all the Town seem happy when
 His prose or verse appears.
They little know the loving heart
 That beats in garret dim,

Or while they daily go to 'Change,
　　What change would be to him!
The Printer's paid—the Paper's paid—
　　The Pressman's pressing, too ;
And while the Author's left to starve,
　　The " Devil," gets his due ;
The Publisher in carriage rolls,
　　And sleeps on feather bed,
　　　　While he that gives
　　　　Them all life, lives
　　In a prison of thought and sorrow,
　　Never daring to think on the morrow ;
For the Bookseller's note, which put off the pay,
　　Will not lighten a creditor's tread,
Nor save from the landlord the few darling books
　　Of the Bondman who writes for his bread.

NOTES.

¹ REMINISCENCE OF FORT CORCORAN.—Henry Watterson, Esq., whose striking articles on "Thomas de Quincey," and "American Song, as illustrated by George P. Morris," in the *National Democratic Quarterly*, have attracted such deserved notice, has been writing some graphic sketches of camp and camp-life about Washington, for the Philadelphia *Press*, over the *nom de plume* of "Asa Trenchard." In one of his lengthiest sketches he gives a most earnest and picturesque description of "the first flag-raising over Federal battlements in the Old Dominion" in the war, and which, as an exciting and interesting historical episode in the career of the gallant Sixty-ninth, cannot be omitted from the chronicle which will record the strength and patriotism which constructed Fort Corcoran. Arriving just in time for "the grand, imposing spectacle," he says:

"As I stood and surveyed the hastily summoned regiment—thirteen hundred of them—some in red flannel shirts, with sleeves rolled up, exposing the grand sinews of brawny arms; some in blue jackets, soiled with the toil of the trenches; some in white flowing havelocks; some in cocked hats, and some bareheaded, it was impossible to repress an audible expression of admiration at the splendid material represented for the work or the glory of war. There the dark brows, lowering from massive foreheads over flashing eyes; there, pale but bleachless cheeks to fear, knit closely to impregnable lips, the craters of flaming and invincible breath, the pride and prowess of representative Ireland, the issue of that spreading Celtic seed which has sown the world with power, stood before me.

"The troops were drawn up in a semicircle, gradually rising within the amphitheatre formed by the mounds of earth-erected batteries, the front files sitting, the next grade stooping, and the rear ranks standing upon the declivity, as it sloped upward toward the 'outer walls,' the whole presenting the spectacle of a circus audience, seen from the centre-post in the ring; this centre-post being a noble shaft from which the banner now waves.

"The group around this 'pillar of light' were Colonel Corcoran (now general), Colonel Hunter (now major-general), of the regular army, Captain Meagher (now brigadier-general), John Savage, volunteer aid to Corcoran, and, of course, 'Asa Trenchard.'

"Now for the ceremony.

"First, Colonel Corcoran introduced Colonel Hunter, who had just been assigned the command of the brigade of the Aqueduct, consisting of the Fifth, Twenty-eighth, and Sixty-ninth New York regiments, making some patriotic allusion to the flag. Colonel Hunter was, of course, received with loud acclaim, when Meagher was called out by the throng. He stepped forward, and made a brief but high-toned and patriotic address, showing the devotion Irishmen should bear to that flag which brought succor to them in Ireland, and to which, upon landing in this country, they swore undivided allegiance. He was heartily applauded throughout.

"John Savage, at the desire of Colonel Corcoran, sung the following song to the air of 'Dixie's Land.' It was written by himself, and is entitled 'The Starry Flag,' which is now identified with the Sixty-ninth.

.　　.　　.　　.　　.　　.　　.　　.　　.

"The enthusiasm which this peculiarly stirring song, with its splendid refrain chorused by thirteen hundred brave voices, aroused, while the Stars and Stripes floated proudly forth from the mast-head in the melting sunset on the sweet breeze from the river, cannot be described. It was electrical. There stood the author himself by the side of Meagher, both symbols of Irish patriotism ; there stood those dauntless men, their brothers in arms and exile ; and there, above all—the stripes vying with the red streaks of the west, and its stars with the silver globes that already began to break through the sky—waved the banner which had come to them when starving, which had protected them when flying, and for whose preservation and perpetuation they now marched to the roll of the national reveille! Well might it awaken those grateful hearts ; and no wonder that when the last thunders of the final verse, roaring like distant artillery, were rising up like vigils around the flag, they broke from their places and surrounded their chief, their orator, their priest, and their poet in a general Irish 'hullabaloo,' as inspiring as a camp-meeting. I must say that it was very hard, between the comic, grotesque scene now presented to the eye, and the earnest, heartfelt associations imaged to the heart, it was difficult to refrain from mingled convulsions of laughter and crying.

"A word or two *apropos* of this song, which I cannot but believe has a future in it. Its origin is not less dramatic than its poetry, and its brief story as interesting as the history of the

' Marseillaise' or the 'Star-Spangled Banner.' It was first written and sung on the war transport 'Marion,' on her perilous route up the Potomac through the masked batteries of the enemy's country. . . . ."—*From Morris & Willis's Home Journal.*

2 " Ich sterbe gern für Freiheit und für Licht,
   Getreu der Fahne der ich zugeschworen."
                                    German Song.

3 " A hundred thousand welcomes."

4 Shane O'Neill, the most powerful Ulster chief of his day, had so harassed the English, and scoffed at all their arts of diplomacy, their offers of nobility and reformatory patronage, that the "government seems to have determined, either by force or otherwise, the northern prince must be destroyed." After living for some years the proud, ferocious, and feared ruler of Ulster, he was at last murdered at a feast given to him by the Scotch Macdonnells, of Antrim, whose sept he had formerly ravaged. The instigator of this foul treachery and slaughter was one Piers, an English officer and agent of the Lord Deputy. He appropriated O'Neill's head, and received for it one thousand marks from his master. " This ghastly head was gibbeted high upon a pole, and long grinned upon the towers of Dublin Castle." For an account of Shane, *vide* Mitchel's *Life of Hugh O'Neill.*

5 Kippure, Castle-Kelly, Bal-mannoch, Cornaun (better known as the old hill of Rollinstown, and at present called Montpelier), See-Finane, &c., are the names of hills which form part of the range of Dublin mountains, and look down into Glan-nis-mole, or "the Vale of Thrushes." Kippure is at the remote end of the valley. The Dodder rises in this hill from three springs, which join a short way down, and thence united, spring into the vale. Kilmosantan is the ruin of a primitive Christian church, situate between the river and the well, and about two hundred yards from the latter. The "Golden Spears" are the two conical mountains of Wicklow, known as the "Sugar Loaves."

The above was originally published in 1848; and afterwards collected into the "Lays of the Fatherland," by the author, in 1850. The kind mention of it by several American critics writing on Irish poetry since, has induced the author to free it as much as possible from the inaccuracies consequent upon a hasty publication originally, and without a glance even at the proof-sheets. It has been altered, and somewhat rewritten—it is to be hoped for the better.

[6] Written upon contemplating Stuart's portrait in the Boston Athenæum.

[7] Suggested by Hübner's picture "The Death of the Poacher." See "Gems from the Düsseldorf Gallery," edited by B. Frodsham, and published by the Appletons.

[8] "I'll change them as the Cyprian fair, she did
To moody oxen," &c.

Amongst the instances recorded by the mythologists of the severity of Venus against such as came under her dislike is, that she transformed the women of Amathus, in Cyprus, into oxen, for their cruelty.

[9] "Above the taxes of official seal,
As Titian was in Venice," &c.

On an occasion of general impost upon the inhabitants of Venice, the Senate, in estimation of the genius of Titian, declared him, and one other alone, exempt from the tax. The other was Sansovino, the statuary and architect.

Apropos of the allusion in the text to Titian's portraits of Charles V., I may quote C. P. Carpani (Notes to *Benvenuto Cellini's Memoirs*): "Charles V. particularly declared himself indebted to him three times for immortality, since he had as often drawn his portrait;" and seeing that his courtiers envied the public favors bestowed on one whose only title was *painter*, he observed to them that "he himself could create dukes, counts, and nobles by hundreds, but that God alone could form a Tiziano." Great homage this of monarchy to mind, and not without a reason it would seem, from the attention drawn to these famous portraits. "It is pretended," says Quatremere de Quincy, alluding, in his "Life of Raffaello," to the statement in the *Lettere Pittoriche*, "that the illusion of the likeness was such that the picture, having been placed near a table, the son of the emperor approached it, in order, as he supposed, to talk with his father on business."

[10] "The Campanero in the southern woods," &c.
"Or like the Tinamou, that lonely bird," &c.

"The Campanero never fails to attract the attention of the passenger; at a distance of nearly three miles you may hear the snow-white bird tolling every four or five minutes, like the distant convent-bell."

"Every now and then, the Maam or Tinamou sends forth one long and plaintive whistle from the depths of the forest, and then stops."—WATERTON's *Wanderings in South America*

SYBIL: A TRAGEDY.

THOMAS SEATON DONOHO,

MY DEAR FRIEND—

IT is now eight years since "Sybil" was written, and six since it was put upon the stage. In committing it to the press I desire to dedicate it to you to mark my regard for you as a poet—though you will persist in keeping your light under a bushel—and my affection for you as the almost daily companion of over four years' residence in Washington. On whom could I more becomingly inflict the dedication of the drama? You were the first to mention it in the public press, even before its production; and the sympathetic sharer in its earlier successes, when the newspapers brought us accounts of the enthusiasm created by the young and brilliant tragic actress—Miss Avonia Jones—then representing the heroine.

I have never seen Miss Jones in the part, but can well imagine how greatly her powerful acting, superadded to her admirable presence, tended to kindle the public to a generous reception of the piece.

It is needless now to recall in detail the too flattering recognition of a majority of the critics—inspired, doubtless, more by enthusiasm for the actress than any knowledge of the author —or the equally unmerited severity of a minor branch of the fraternity. Leaving the latter in the hands of the audiences, I offer sincere acknowledgments to the former. In this connection my thanks are especially due to that fine poet and wit, George D. Prentice, who, unknown to me save by reputation, acted as mediator on behalf of Authors' Rights, on an exciting occasion, to which the following letter, addressed to a New York journal, refers :—

"WASHINGTON, Oct. 31, 1858.

"In your paper of yesterday's date the article on the drama contained the following :

"'John Savage's play of "Sybil," after running with great enthusiasm, has been withdrawn in consequence of the remonstrances of the family where the chief incident occurred. It is not, perhaps, known that it is founded on an event which happened in Kentucky. Its dramatic success, however, will, no doubt, induce Mr. Savage to try again on a less dangerous subject.'

"Permit me to say that 'Sybil' has not been withdrawn. The acting of it was postponed one night in Louisville, out of respect to the request of the Governor of Kentucky, and for reasons which the leading journals of Louisville then thought sufficient. Owing to certain criticisms having preceded the play, and to the probably injudicious announcement of it by the manager in Louisville, it was thought by some persons to reflect upon a respectable family in that State, some incidents of the play having been suggested by a notable passage in the criminal and domestic history of Kentucky. Upon this supposition the play was, after some negotiation, suppressed on the night for which it was first announced in Louisville. Upon its representation, however, 'Sybil' was declared to be a fiction. The Louisville Courier, while paying it such compliments as I would blush to reproduce, repudiated the idea that it was a representation of facts, and said: 'Let it rather be called "Sybil," with no attempt to invest it with the terrors of a local incident, which it does not attempt to portray according to history or tradition.' I willingly accept the proposition of the Courier, for as Mr. G. D. Prentice previously said in his Journal, 'The author, ——, knew nothing, and sought to know nothing, as to the life and death of ——, except from tradition, and he relied partly upon these, but far more upon his own fancy and invention, in the composition of the piece, his whole purpose being to render the play, both in incident and in language, as effective as he possibly could.'

"The representation of 'Sybil' was attended by a most remarkable success (as the papers testify). Miss Avonia Jones was re-engaged for three nights, and performed it each night with great enthusiasm on the part of the audience, and increased honor to herself as an actress of wonderful original powers. The details of the 'excitement' I omit, but submit the above facts in explanation and correction of your paragraph, which was, no doubt, based upon the articles announcing the temporary postponement of 'Sybil' in Louisville.

"Yours respectfully,

"JOHN SAVAGE."

This letter is reprinted in justice to myself, especially as lengthy "Statements" were put forth suggesting an imputation on my motives in using the material which furnished the key note of the drama. William Gilmore Simms wrote two novels on the subject; Charles Fenno Hoffman, I learn, also made it the theme of a novel. Our friend, Clifton W. Tayleure, drew a melodrama from it, and the excitement jointly produced by the representation of "Sybil" and the Statements against it made me acquainted with the fact that other dramas and stories had been founded upon it. With much more justice might the motives of these authors be impugned, if any such imputation be warranted by the use of facts which have gone into history. The late distinguished author of the "Blithedale Romance," in his preface to that work—fearful lest readers might confound his romance with the persons and scenes of a certain community—stated, that while availing himself of actual reminiscences to give a more life-like tint to the creation of his fancy, he so used scenes, incidents, and persons, that " the creatures of his brain might play their phantasmagorical antics without exposing them to too close a comparison with the actual events of real lives." The same, in a still greater degree, is true of the use of material in "Sybil."

I would not willingly wound the feelings of any one, much less those already seared by tender connection with the victim of a foul deed. It does not follow, that because a dramatist, or other writer, takes certain incidents as the basis of a work, he may not produce them by the means of characters totally different from those concerned in their actual perpetration. Natures of a directly opposite stamp may, for all dramatic, poetic, and moral purposes, be most suitable to heighten the effect of such acts or incidents. It is so in the present instance. Between the chief Statement, by its own showing, and the story as

conveyed in this piece, there is but one point of similarity—the
fact of an assassination.   There is no resemblance between the
contrivers and perpetrators, as respectively drawn ; the character of the victim in the one, is as opposite to that of the other
as noonday and midnight : and the attempt to create an identity between them is as unjust to the memory of the actual, as
to the dramatist who now presents the acted, character.   The
unfortunate use of a name found in a stray newspaper article,
which first suggested the theme, and retained in Simms'
novel—the only one on the subject I was then aware of—and
to which I was further indebted, gave a clue to a supposed
identity not to be found on even a casual examination.
This name has been changed ; and I would not now allude to
the matter at all, but that when represented, the critics, otherwise but too kind, taking their cue from the original " excitement," as mentioned above, constantly refer to it ; and on giving it to the press, I could not run the risk of having my
silence construed into even a remote acquiescence in the injus-
tice of the statements, so far as they refer to " Sybil" or its
author.

    After such an unpleasant, though necessary digression, I
may be permitted to refresh myself with memories more suitable to my nature—thoughts conjured up by reminiscences of
our homes in Washington, and of days spent with you on the
hills of Maryland and Virginia and along the then delightful
banks of the Potomac.   The mention of Washington evokes
memories of an eventful and instructive, even if laborious
period of my life, and the social and generous companionship
of many dear friends : it calls up the hospitable and brilliant
board of John F. Coyle ; the serene enjoyment and unflagging
interest of the statesmen-groups gathered around our benign
host of Strawberry Knoll, Mr. Kingman ; the trusty good nature of my friend of many years, Dr. Thomas Antisell ; the
pleasant hours in the artistic *salôn* of J. C. McGuire ; besides,
a host, out of which it would be ungracious to individualize,
many of whom have since gone forth from rival camps, and
found a resting-place, once again, side by side—in death.   You
know my sense of duty to my country—and I will not dwell
on that theme here lest the passions, which mortality cannot

shake off, might arise to crush out the beauty of the past. In dedicating this little book to you, I could not repress a tribute to days past, and to the friends who contributed so much to make them joyous and happy.

   With great esteem,
     I beg to subscribe myself,
        Your friend,
           JOHN SAVAGE.

NEW ORLEANS, Sept. 14, 1864.

DRAMATIS PERSONÆ.

EUSTACE CLIFDEN.

RUFUS WOLFE.

OLD ACTON.

WILLIAM ACTON.

MR. LOWE.

BARNABAS.

LANDLORD OF THE RED HEIFER

GENTLEMEN.

SYBIL HARDY.

MRS. HARDY.

MAUDE CLIFDEN.

JANETTE.

SCENE.— *In the State of Kentucky.*

TIME.—*First decade of the Nineteenth Century.*

SYBIL.

ACT I.

SCENE I.—*A Club-room, handsomely furnished.*

RUFUS WOLFE, BARNABAS, MR. LOWE, *and several gentlemen, reading papers, &c.*

Wolfe. Our new member is not stirring yet.

1st Gent. No—thanks to your sleight of hand last night. I should not be surprised if he didn't stir for a month.

2d Gent. I never saw a jollier initiation !

Bar. He may not be so jolly when he's sober.

Wolfe. Oh, he won't remember his assaults on our friend Lowe : eh, Cardinal ?

Lowe. But I'll take care he shall.

Wolfe. He's young and inexperienced ; and the deeds of wine evaporate with its effects.

Bar. I never saw a wilder fellow in his cups.

Wolfe. I thought him rather serious. Did not *you,* Cardinal ? (*To Lowe.*)

Lowe. I tell you what, gentlemen, I'll resign my presidency of this club, if I'm not protected against every dare-devil, who, inspired by Wolfe's mad humors, plays off his drunken jokes on me—I will.

2

All. No—no. Ha ! ha !

Lowe. I will, gentlemen,—I do protest I will,—if it even shatters the unity of the society—I will.

Several. Oh, no.

Enter EUSTACE CLIFDEN.

1*st Gent.* Our new member !

Wolfe. Good morning, Clifden.

Several. Good morning. (*Salute him.*)

Clif. Good morning, gentlemen. (*Goes to Lowe.*) Mr. Lowe, I am very glad to see you here ; it saves me the necessity of calling upon you.

Wolfe. Bravo, Clifden !

Lowe. Calling upon me, sir ! for what, Mr. Clifden ?

Wolfe. For what ? Oh, innocent Cardinal—for satisfaction, to be sure.

Lowe. Sir, I'll resign this moment.

Clif. Allow me, Mr. Lowe, to apologize for my rudeness to you last night. I was not conscious of it, I assure you ; and I am indebted to the kindness of some friends for the information this morning.

Lowe. You were rude, sir, that you were.

Clif. I am sorry for it, Mr. Lowe ; sorry that I should, without cause, affront any man, but more especially one whose position should be sufficient protection against insult. I sincerely apologize.

1*st Gent.* I should think an apology from any member of the club, for any reason, decidedly inexcusable.

Several. Decidedly—decidedly.

Clif. (*calmly.*) It was, sir, thoroughly unwarrantable on my part to offer a rudeness to you ; and I say again, I apologize.

Lowe. It was unwarrantable ; but, sir, since you have

the manliness to apologize, I give you my hand (*Lowe and Clifden shake hands*), and I hope you have safely survived the pains of initiation.

Wolfe. Does the head ache still?

Bar. Are the nerves disordered?

1st Gent. Hand shaky?

Lowe. In a word, my good sir, are you washed out? Ha! ha!

Clif. No, but to say truth, I feel inexpressibly ashamed.

Bar. and 1st and 2d Gent. Ha! ha! he!

Wolfe. Nonsense, man.

Clif. I am very sorry you persuaded me to join your club.

Wolfe. Persuade! 'Twas scarcely possible to avoid it. Every young lawyer, to be recognized, must go through it.

Bar. Your regrets are treasonable.

Clif. I feel them, nevertheless. I must have been wild, if what I hear be true.

1st Gent. Slightly elevated, that's all.

Clif. I never was *slightly elevated* before, and, club or no club, I never will be again.

Wolfe. We have all said the same thing once.

Clif. I cannot, even now, understand it. I drank but little wine.

Lowe. Precious little. Ha! ha! But you may thank Wolfe's adroitness in mingling the liquors.

Clif. What!

Wolfe. Pshaw, Clifden, you were never born for a Puritan. You are a fellow for fun, high frolic, and the enjoyment of the earth.

1st Gent. Certainly, and if a man may forget himself

and be mad for a night, it is that night when he is admitted to the Temple of Anacreon.   Don't take it so seriously.

Bar. All over now, you know.

Lowe. You are young, sir, and likely to be abused ; take the advice of an older man—these gay fellows are making fun of you, Mr. Clifden.

Several. Ha ! ha !   Good !

1st Gent. Very good, your reverence !

Lowe. He ! he ! he ! you puppies, I shall leave you to your politics.   (*Going.*) I see young Acton is in the field against you (*to Wolfe*) ; take care lest you force me into the opposition.   (*Exit, followed by the gents.*)

Wolfe. Yes, Acton is in the field against me, and I need the services of all my friends.   I count on you, Clifden.

Clif. Whatever I can, I will do ; but—

Wolfe. No *buts.*   You are already popular, and the time is auspicious.   The life of a man almost depends on his first marked effort.   You are just admitted to the bar, and with your reputation as a speaker here, something is expected of you.   There could not be a better opportunity to distinguish yourself.   You must meet Acton in discussion.

Clif. Me ?   He will need a stronger opponent.   Why not do this yourself?

Wolfe. I long for nothing better, but I cannot be everywhere.   I'll seek him in time.   When do you leave town ?

Clif. To-day ; within the hour.

Bar. So soon?

Wolfe. Why, I expected you to dinner ; Mrs. Wolfe will be disappointed.

Clif. I am sorry to deny myself the pleasure, but urgent matters—very urgent indeed—demand my presence.

Bar. But a day or two?

Clif. I wrote to—to—my sister—

Wolfe. What of that. A little delay will make you the more welcome. Let the girls wait; don't be a boy always. You will meet some excellent fellows, see how we commence the campaign, and so forth.

Bar. Strong temptations.

Clif. Yes, but I confess to my boyhood, and will prove my manhood by resisting your temptations.

Wolfe. Stubborn. Well, I will write to you then. I have a strong desire—apart from my own interests—to see you in the field.

Clif. Thank you, I shall hear from you. Adieu.

Wolfe. }
Bar. } Adieu.   (*Shake hands.*)   [*Exit* CLIF.

Wolfe. He does not know his own powers. We must bring him fully out.

Bar. 'Tis not so easy to meet Acton. What is there against him?

Wolfe. His pamphlet. Every line a man writes is political capital for his enemies. Then, he is obscure, that's certain. Little known among the masses, and for a good reason—he does not mix with them; he is a haughty aristocrat, a man who only knows the people when he wants their votes.

Bar. Is that actually the case?

Wolfe. Simpleton! We must make it so.

Bar. Oh—ah—yes.

Wolfe. It may be, or may not be, what is the difference to us. That he is shy and reserved is, I understand,

2*

a fact. Well, it is just as likely he is so from pride as
any thing else, do you see? Perhaps he's a fellow of
delicate feelings! So much the better. People don't
like fellows of delicate feelings. Ha! ha! Delicate
feelings are very unpopular things. They alone would
go hard against him. If we could have him persuaded
to wear kid gloves it would save us a few thousand.
Kid gloves are not popular; if any thing, they are more
ruinous than the feelings aforesaid. Then he is cautious
of taverns. Couldn't the popular eye discover a demijohn in his study—ay, could it! Ha! ha! Pride, tender feelings, kid gloves, private demijohn—political
death, certain. Come along, Barnabas, old boy, we
must let the people know of these things.

[Exit Wolfe and Bar.

Scene II.—On the skirt of a wood overlooking the ruined village
of Eaglemont.

Enter Old Acton and William Acton.

Old A. (*contemplating the scene*). We are here
again, William; here, without a single companion of all
those old ones who were associated with that once dear
village; and yet we are not without some of the old
friends—the old trees and rocks and hills are about us.
Bless me, I feel the former life, if not the old feelings;
yet, what a change. Five years have done it all. Five
years only, yet what an eternity it seems.

Acton. I see no sign of human life.

Old A. Indeed, it looks as if there were none. Shall
we descend into the valley and inquire further?

Acton. Why, sir, further? Here, it seems to me, we
can

Behold enough for melancholy thought.
See—yonder ruins of my father's home ;
There I first wak'd to this now weary world ;
There was a child ; there sprang from youth to man,
Beneath the touch of Love's delicious hopes—
Hopes which, alas, that same old roof saw blasted.

    Old A. And there my school-house stands, as years
        ago,
Save that it glooms with age and loneliness.
I could embrace my dear old fav'rite oaks !
They seem to welcome me with outstretched arms ;
Or, it may be, they wave me from the scene.
How much do they recall !   Their shapes have grown
Into my heart with the old books I've read
Beneath their patriarchal shelter.

    Acton (musing). How brief a term makes life deso-
        lation ?
Why shall we wonder that no vestige marks
The spots where stood the cities of the past ;
When here, what was, a few short years ago,
A thriving, robust village, is but now
A bundle of old gables ?

    Old A.   Discontent
Between a couple of families, my son,
Has sundered towns more populous than this.
This very cause made you the first to leave.

    Acton. Yes, but not willingly I left my home—
A loving heart, a cruel, brutal fate
Drove me from out my native sanctuary.

    Old A. Well, I rejoice that it was so.   The necessity
which expelled you was the mother of a glorious future.
It brought out the manhood that was in you, and will
crown your name with honor.

Acton. Yet, sir, I would gladly exchange all—
All that I am, all that I hope to be,
For the dear dreams that fill'd my boyhood's home.

Old A. No, no. To-morrow, when you return to the
political action you have entered upon, you will feel
how idle was the sentiment, seeming so natural to you
now. What? If this was the scene of your sports and
love, was it not also the theatre of your denial, your
strife, and bitter humiliation : would you feel those pangs
anew ?

Acton. No, no ; do not remind me. See there—see !
(*Catching Old Acton's arm.*) Dost not descry a female
        figure ? There—
Below the copse : 'Tis lost now. There, again,
Anear the margin of the lake it stands.
It looks like her ! Could it be Margaret !

Old A. I see.

Acton. Stay, father—I would speak with her. (*Going,
Old A. detains him.*)

Old A. Why should ye speak—have you any thing
pleasant to communicate to each other ? You are un-
reasonable, my son. (*William subdued.*) And tell me,
William, is it still in your mind to marry Margaret
Cooper.

Acton. Oh no, sir—no ! How could you suppose it !

Old A. I do not suppose it ; therefore I say you are
unkind, cruel, my son, in your attempt to see that woman
you believed to be her. You have no business with her.

Acton. Father—my more than father, you are right. I
deserve reproof. 'Twas a blind impulse. I am a boy
still. Let us leave this place.

Old A. Forget these dreams. All your thoughts
need other direction now. Your antagonist if less able,

is a more practised politician, and works upon a very perfect organization.

Acton. I was not made for political strife.

Old A. It is the very sphere of action that will attract you from the chimeras of fancy and boyhood. When you have a seat in Congress you will, in the expansive field before you, forget that such a little village as this beneath us has ever been on a map. Come, William, to-morrow will see us harnessed for the fight.

[*Exit* OLD ACTON, *leading* WILLIAM ACTON.

SCENE III.—*A Room in Clifden's Country Cottage, neatly furnished.*

MAUDE CLIFDEN, JANETTE, *seated.*

Maude. Brother Eustace is outstaying his time. I am the more anxious for his return, because I thought he left us in rather a melancholy mood. Did you not think so ?

Jan. Do not fear but he will keep his appointment. Even if he would disappoint us, there are other attractions in this neighborhood from which he would not willingly remain distant. (*Taking a book from the table.*) See there, Maude.

Maude (*reading from fly-leaf*). "Sybil Hardy." Why, what a rogue—he never mentioned he had met her.

Jan. Which only proves the truth of what I say.

Maude. Where did you find this ?

Jan. On his dressing-table.

Maude. Ah, Eustace, we have found you out. Well, I'm glad of it—ain't you ? There will be some reason for his staying with us now—we have scarcely seen him since he went studying that stupid law.

Jan. I would it were some other than our melancholy neighbor.

Maude. Why, Janette, I do believe you are jealous.

Jan. If I were I would not show it, Maude.

Maude. Ha! ha! why 'twas but yesterday you said jealousy was the only thing a woman could not hide.

Jan. Well—yes, a woman who was in love.

Maude. Of course, a woman could not be jealous without being in love.

Jan. But she might love without being jealous.

Maude. And that is what my cousin could not do.

Jan. (*who has retired towards the window.*) Here he is. Look how he steals along, as though he were going to a friend's funeral; and now he stops, and dallies, and looks behind him, as if expecting some one.

Maude. Does he not look handsome—so tall and graceful.

Jan. There's a cloud upon his brow.

Maude. We will dispel it. Here he comes.

Enter EUSTACE CLIFDEN.

Welcome, brother. (*Embraces him.*)

Clif. Ah—dear Maude. Has Cousin Janette no welcome for me? She forgets the customs of our childhood, when she would cling to me as a vine round the trellis.

Jan. And Eustace then told all his secrets to his little cousin.

Maude. Yes, indeed. Ah, ha! brother, we have found you out. (*Clifden puzzled.*)

Jan. (*Showing the book.*) Eh, Master Cunning!

Clif. So, Miss Pry-about. Well, Coz, kiss me and I'll tell you all about it.

Maude. There now, make up. (*Pulling them togeth-*

*er, Clifden kisses Janette, who offers coy resistance—
they all sit.)*

Jan. You did not tell us of your visits to Miss Hardy.

Clif. You did not tell me that such a beauty adorned
the vicinity.

Jan. Do you think *her* a beauty?

Maude. Of course he does. (*To him.*) Well, how
did you meet her?

Clif. Well, when home last week I went out shoo:
ing—

Jan. And was struck yourself.

Maude. Now, Janette.

Clif. I went out shooting, or to shoot; and, toiling
after game in the wood, started, by a lucky shot, a
young lady from the thicket: common courtesy com-
manded me to apologize—

Maude. Of course.

Clif. And see that the frighted creature was not hurt—

Jan. Or pierced through the heart.

Clif. She, however, avoided me.

Jan. Of course, to drag you after her.

Maude. Oh, Janette, how can you.

Clif. She hastened, with becoming delicacy, to the
open path. I followed, and though she declined my service as escort, I continued, gently insisting, until she
came within sight of her cottage.

Jan. Did you not go home with her?

Clif. No; but on my return through the wood I
found—fortunate discovery—her veil, which I restored
next day; and made bold to borrow that book—and
that's all.

Maude. Quite an adventure; how could you keep it
from us?

Jan. It was too charming for expression. Why, he's blushing, as I live. Ha! ha!

Clif. Tut, tut, Janette—nonsense!—just heated with walking.

Jan. Heated, indeed, at a snail's pace. You sauntered along, and looked from side to side, as though thinking whether you'd go over to Miss Hardy's or come here; and sighed—oh, dear! you could be heard half a mile away.

Clif. Sigh—oh, ridiculous. (*Sighs.*) What do you know of the lady—eh, Maude? Janette, who is she?

Jan. She's a mystery of some sort or another. Maybe an exiled queen, good lack, or she wants to be thought one.

Maude. Oh, Janette!

Jan. Well, is it not true? Does she not carry herself like a queen, and is she not as proud and stately as if she would remind us all we were beneath her.

Clif. She certainly does look queenly.

Jan. A tragedy-queen!

Maude. I'm sure she is unhappy.

Jan. I don't believe in her unhappiness at all. She is too proud to be so unhappy as you think.

Clif. Might not pride itself be the very cause or the effect of unhappiness?

Jan. But are we to sympathize with it?

Clif. (*to Maude*). How long has she resided hereabout?

Maude. She and her mother came some two years ago—just after you left us to study law. They bought the Widow Davis's cottage, and fixed themselves and a few servants very comfortably. Mrs. Hardy is a good-natured body.

Jan. And very silly. I don't believe she is the mother of our queen at all.

Clif. (*to Maude*). And the daughter?—

Maude. She is not very sociable. She is seldom seen by casual visitors; and, indeed, has not been here more than four or five times. Janette thinks her proud, but I do not. Her manners are dignified; but there is such a look of sadness in her eyes, that I cannot help thinking her unhappy. Probably she has been disappointed in love.

Jan. Maude is making a heroine of her. One day she is a recluse; another, she has been engaged, and her lover played false and deserted her—

Maude. No, I said he might have been killed in a duel, as any man might be for such a woman.

Clif. Bravo—bravo—Maude!

Jan. 'Tis well you're not a man, Maude, or our trage-dy-queen would help to kill our cousin.

Maude. Is she not beautiful? Is she not, brother? They say, too, that she is intellectual and learned.

Clif. Who says?

Jan. Who, but old Mrs. Fisher, and solely because she saw her fixing a basketful of books on her shelves.

Maude. Why, Judge Weldon told me he spoke with her, and that he never believed a woman could be so sensible before.

Jan. That only shows what a poor judge he is.

Maude. But Miss Hardy *is* sensible. I have spoken with her myself.

Jan. Well, she's old enough to have the sense of two young women at least.

Clif. Old? the lady I mean is certainly not old.

Maude. Cousin Janette is only teazing, thinking that

3

our lovely, but melancholy friend, has bewitched you. She is not old, cannot be more than one or two and twenty.

Jan. And is not that old? you are but sixteen, Maude, and I'm not eighteen—I'm sure Miss Hardy is twenty-five if she's a day.

Maude. Come, come, Janette, if you stay another minute you'll have Miss Hardy a gaunt old lady, with a few teeth and a pair of spectacles.

[*Exit* MAUDE *and* JANETTE, *laughing.*

Clif. Maude is right—Sybil's truly beautiful!
Oh, why have I not known her before now.
The moment I but glanced into her eyes
I read my destiny.   I look'd and loved.
From the creative heaven of her face
A whole new world leaped into my heart;
A world teeming with a thousand hopes,
Each taking inspiration from that face.
I've heard, but never felt its truth till now,
That persons of congenial souls exchange
Themselves on first collision of their eyes.
She has my being, and to win her not
Is to abandon and forsake myself.
How much I've lived within a week, and yet,
My very strength of feeling calls up fears
That goad me with a reckless speed to know,
If I may not in her heart's empire dwell,
As she fills up the whole domain of mine.

[*Music as act drop falls*

ACT II.

SCENE I.—*A wood. A paper mark on trunk of a tree.* SYBIL HARDY *discovered in the foreground firing at the mark with a pistol. After firing,* SYBIL *looks with calm eagerness at the effect.*

Sybil. Thank heaven, I fail not ; each unerring shot
Is certain intimation of revenge,
And daily gives me courage to live on. (*Moves.*)
Without this all-sustaining, grateful hope,
The solitude I breathe were death : and death
That might have been a heav'nly gift, ere fled
My happy childhood trembling from my heart
(As though affrighted by its haughty blood),
Would now be that most unforgiving curse
This wilful, woful, wretched brain could bear.
Five years, like monumental marbles rise
Above my girlish beauty, and record
The gnawing consciousness of coarse deceit,
The bitter anguish of defrauded hopes,
Mocked aims ; the loss of name, position, love ;
The loss of all those dear amenities
That should have been the guerdon and the guide,
The life itself of the proud, withered youth beneath.
    (*Weeps.*)
'Tis strange these maddening, these blighting years
Have left untouched one corner of my brain :
That here, far distant from the village where
I ruled, already in my youth a queen ;
Far from my friends' condole, my foes' contempt,
That here unknown, unfriended—save by one,

A doting mother, whose unwavering heart
Still dulls her ears to censure, and whose eyes
Still fling a tearful glory round her child—
I teach the woman in her pallid prime
T' avenge my girlhood's blushing trustfulness.
(*Starts.*) Here is my neighbor whom I fear to meet,
And yet there is a restless sympathy,
Some dread, electric chain that brings us close.
I would avoid him : would that he would me.
Oh heaven ! that I were younger by five years.   (*Conceals the pistol.*)

Enter EUSTACE CLIFDEN.

Clifden. Ah, Miss Hardy, pardon my intrusion.   It was unintentional.

Sybil. Your presence is pardonable, Mr. Clifden, but scarcely your excuse.

Clif. I feared my presence would but awaken a disdain, that one of us, at least, should bear unanswered.

Sybil. Sir, I fear you understand yourself less than you even understand me.   I shall relieve your feelings by withdrawing.   (*Going.*)

Clif. Stay, Miss Hardy.   (*Goes after her.*)
Sybil, dear Sybil, do not leave me thus :
Hear me but for a moment.   Well I know,
After what has transpired, that I am
Bound to your pity, mercy, or contempt.
But an absorbing love like mine fears not
The self-reproaches of a callous pride,
That tames the blood of those who think they love.
Love is a slave, yet those who think they have
Timely control of all its dang'rous ecstasies

Have never loved—or have no power to love.
You bid me go, but *I* dare not depart.

   Sybil. Clifden, 'twere wrong to listen yet again,
To what 'twere better I had never heard.
I must not—better for us both I should not.
You found *me* here in solitude.   To me
You were a stranger.   Strangers each to each.
You nothing know of me :—of you, I nothing.
Let us be friends as neighbors :—seek no more :
If not, then let us part.

   Clif.   Know nothing of you !
Sybil, ask your heart.

   Sybil (*energetically*). Ha! sir! what mean you ?
What can you know of me?

   Clif. (*Sybil betrays much anxiety.*) Much !
These solemn cloistered woods are witnesses—
These oaks that eloquently stretch their arms
To heaven, and bless you in their sheltering calm—
These my loved rivals for affection, feel
In thy dear presence what I proudly know ;
That you among earth's fairest are alone—
Alone in beauty, in intellect alone !
This do I know and feel ; and is not this
All that I ever wish to know.

   Sybil (*staggering and faint*). Thank heaven ! (*Aside.*)

   Clif. (*supporting her*). You are ill—

   Sybil. Do not be alarmed, I (*regains her position*)—
I am better now (*disengages herself*) ; I am subject to
such attacks, and they form a sufficient reason, Mr. Clifden, why I should not distress strangers with them.

   Clif. Strangers ! but I to whom love makes you all—
To whom the hope—

           3*

Sybil.   Hope !—hope nothing from me.
I would not have you hope in vain.

Clif. That kind desire assures me that I may not.

Sybil. You deceive yourself——Do not question me
This meeting has awakened in my brain
Many a dreary thought.   Again I say,
As, Eustace Clifden, I before have said,
I am divided, cut off from the world.
How or why it matters not : it is so.

Clif. Your destiny, dim as you paint its path,
But throbs my heart with willingness to share
And soothe it.

Sybil.   That can never be.

Clif. If you but knew my heart—

Sybil. Enough that I do know my own ; and it
Has but one prayer, for peace ; one passion, and that—

Clif. Is—relieve me, Sybil—but say not you love
Another.

Sybil (scornfully). Love ! no sir, I do not love.
Happily I am free from such a weakness.

Clif. Is that a weakness which inspires all strength,
And gives the only purpose life possesses ?

Sybil. When we met I hoped I had met a friend,
And now I grieve that we have ever met.

Clif. I pray, thee, Sybil, do not wrong me in this
          decision.

Sybil. I do not.   Your worth, your generous soul
And loving nature well I know.
You've offered me far more than I deserve ;
More than I dare accept—

Clif.   Then you would—

Sybil.   Ay :
Were it possible I could ever wed,

I do not know a mortal unto whom
I could so well my best affections trust,
As to you, Eustace : but that cannot be.
There is between us a broad barrier—

Clif. What barrier can come between us
That we ourselves will not ! Here face to face,
Before the smiling face of heaven, what
Can separate us. This barrier, Sybil,
Is but some gloomy mountain of the mind,
Which I can speedily surmount. Whate'er
Stout heart and willing hand can do, I'll do.
What is it ?

Sybil. The very question deeper makes the gulf
And lifts the barrier higher : it opes
A breach that might an angry ocean bed.
Reveal it ! Powers of Innocence and Truth (*aside*)
I cannot, dare not. 'Tis enough I ne'er
Can listen to your prayer—or be your wife.

Clif. Sybil—

Sybil. Nor the wife of any man.
I entreat thee ask no more :—you'll drive me mad.
Farewell, Eustace, farewell. (*Going, he follows.*) Do
      not follow
If you love me. We must not meet again.
(*He droops and kisses her hand.*) Farewell.

                    [*Exit* SYBIL.

SCENE II.—*Street.*

Enter RUFUS WOLFE, BARNABAS, *and* MR. LOWE.

Wolfe. But, Lowe, my dear friend, you do not mean
to come out for Acton, eh ? I really cannot do without
your services.

3

Lowe. Well, the fact is, I have no settled political opinions : I have not made up my mind on the one hand, and on the other I believe young Mr. Acton, whom I have met sometimes, to be a very good and clever fellow.   Indeed, I think he would be a very serious addition to our club.

Bar. A very *serious* addition, no doubt.

Lowe. Well, I've been thinking, Wolfe, if I had two votes I would give you one each ; but as I have only one, I have almost determined not to hurt either of my friends by using it.

Wolfe. A most unpatriotic speech—

Bar. And opposed to the best interests of the community ; for if you are not wholly with us, you are against us.   Besides, every one should know the right side and use the privilege of citizenship.

Lowe. But, my gay fellows, I really do not know the points at issue, if any, between the parties.

Bar. Pshaw ! go for your friends, and hang the points at issue.   You know our friend Wolfe.   Everybody knows him ; while Acton, on the contrary, is but of a few years' growth amongst us.   It is nothing but personal ambition with him.

Lowe. I think you mistake the young man, or I do.

Wolfe (motioning to Barnabas). Our worthy president is right, but he will pledge us his silence ; for next to his aid for us, is his silence for our antagonist.

Lowe. Ah, Colonel, very graceful, I assure you, but you overrate me as much as Barnabas underrates Acton.

Wolfe. Acton's address is written well and artfully.

Bar. Rather puritanical.

Wolfe. You must admit, Cardinal, my good friend, that he comes rather disadvantageously into the field just now.   A few years hence and he might have an opening.

Lowe. Well, well, to be sure ; but a man may as well commence some time, you know.   By the way, have you any objection to meet him ?

Wolfe. Not at all, but quite the contrary.   It is no reason, because we are political rivals, why we should not be personal friends.

Lowe. I meet the old gentleman this evening, at his lodgings at the *Red Heifer.*   If you agree to call for me, I will be happy to prepare him for an introduction.

Wolfe. Certainly—what say you, Barnabas ?

Bar. I am agreed.

Lowe. At eight (*going*).

Both. Eight.   [*Exit* LOWE.

Wolfe. Then we can the better see the mettle of this stripling, and judge what strength we must put forth.

Bar. His friends are enthusiastic, and busy everywhere.

Wolfe. And mine are nearly asleep.   We must arouse them.   Come.   [*Exeunt.*

SCENE III.—*Room in the Red Heifer Inn.*

WILLIAM ACTON *seated thoughtfully at a table.*

Acton. Five years of what the world calls success
Have passed ; yet still my rustic memories cling
About my honors with a saddening gloom.
'Tis only action makes the present light ;
Each resting moment brings the weighty past.
Her image ever pleads before my thought
With strange prophetic feeling—now bright as dawn,
Pure in the opening bounty of its light ;

And then, as dismal as a shadow cast
Across some ravine where a hidden stream
Gurgles and moans with wretched energy.
Two images of one, and how unlike each other.
One, like the eagle soaring in the sun,
Its brave soul bounding with the air of heaven ;
And proud eye looking down a scorn on earth.
The other, gloomy as the great bird, caged,
Tattered in plumage and with broken wing,
Fettered in spirit, and its eyes grown weak
With madly gazing at obscurity.

Enter OLD ACTON.

Old A. (*aside*). Pondering still, ever on the sad old
    theme—
(*Slaps him on the back.*) Dreaming of fame and fortune
    in your grasp ?
    Acton. (*Sighs.*) The scene we witnessed yesterday has
    dragg'd
All the old associations up.
They crowd the glories of the present out.
    Old A. But you must leave the past where it left you
I tell thee, William, that your loss in youth
Was the most fortunate of all your gains,
Great as they have been.
    Acton.   My gain was great, indeed,
In having you adopt me as your son.
    Old A. Your own strong character has been your
    crown.
Had your wild passions won a tame success
You'd soon have sunk into the dull routine
And healthy torpor of the farmer's life.
The subtle knowledge of yourself were lost,

Which only disappointment made you find.
The raging troubles of a blighted heart
Comfort themselves in the disguise of pride,
Which with the insight into life love breeds,
Gives talent concentration, and makes man
Strong to bear up 'gainst nature's keen delusions.
The time will come you'll wonder this girl e'er
Could have been dear to you.

    Acton.   Never, never.

    Old. A. The passion of the boy, is but a boy passion.

    Acton. My mind had not then reached the easy width
Which yields an entrance to the grosser thoughts
Of years. My heart alone was living then ;
And lived but in the thought of her.

    Old A. Years bring grossness only to the gross.
Had you your rival's knowledge of the world
You might have been successful. Simply he
Held up the mirror to her vanity
And pleased her with herself. He fed her with
Her own ambition ; little troubling him
With her affections, which he soon found were
All bonded to her brain. This made her bold
And confident in fancied strength that proved
Her total weakness. He knew her nature.

    Acton. It maddens me to hear the villain's name.
I'd freely give up all—all I have won,
All that you fondly hope I'll win, to know,
Where at this moment I could place my hand
Upon his throat.

    Old A.   Would that restore her
To her peace of mind, or obliterate
Your memories ?

    Acton. No, but it would drag

The libertine from bold obscurity,
To public retribution and disgrace.

Old A. Which would with equal scandal fall upon
His wretched victim. See what you would do.

Acton. 'Tis true. Father, I yield to you, my best,
My wisest, and most loving counsellor.

Old A. 'Tis sad, and false in spirit as in deed,
To know and feel society's so formed,
That we must often chain the tongue to save
That very one, whose wrongs the loudest call
For honest vindication.

Enter MR. LOWE.

Welcome, Mr. Lowe, welcome.

Acton. I feared you had forgotten us.

Lowe. Not so ; indeed, my dear sir, I remembered
you so well that I refused to take any side in politics lest
I might injure your prospects.

Acton. How so ?

Lowe. Well, by taking part with Wolfe, or by adopt-
ing your side, in not being able to expound it.

Old A. Could you expound the opposition ?

Lowe. By my word, I did not think of that : but
you can have an opportunity of hearing an authority on
that head if you so desire.

Acton. The more we know of it the better shall we be
able to refute it.

Lowe. You have never met your opponent Colonel
Wolfe ?

Acton. Not to my knowledge.

Lowe. He knows your reputation ; and as you are
both lawyers, and understand the courtesy due to rivalry,
I asked him to stop here for me as he was passing.

Old A. You did well, friend Lowe, to initiate the contest with a friendly feeling.

Enter LANDLORD *of Red Heifer.*

Landlord (uneasily). Squire—

Old A. What's the matter?

Land. The place is a' most besieged with a gang of fellows belonging to the t'other side. They'll ruin me 'fore election day comes on. There won't be left a toddy in the town. (*Hurrahs outside.*) There they go, and Colonel Wolfe himself's at the head of them.

Old A. Colonel Wolfe—Mr. Lowe's friend—show him up.

Land. Wolfe! (*in amazement*) up here!

Old A. Yes, up here; and give his friends good welcome down below. [*Exit* LANDLORD.] Ha! ha! the landlord, who's an ardent partisan of ours, can scarcely reconcile Wolfe's presence in the enemy's headquarters.

Enter RUFUS WOLFE *and* BARNABAS.

Lowe (meeting them). Up to time, sirs. (*Addressing all parties.*) Now, gentlemen, introduce yourselves as fearless rivals ought.

BARNABAS *smirkingly approaches* OLD ACTON, *who extends his hand.*

Old A. Welcome, gentlemen.

Wolfe (advancing to Wm. Acton). Mr. William Acton, I believe; I am Colonel Wolfe.

Acton. (suddenly withdrawing his extended hand and peering steadfastly at Wolfe). You, sir, Rufus Wolfe?—You? (*General surprise.*)

Wolfe.　　　　　　What is this?

4

I *am* Colonel Wolfe ; and you, sir—
Are you not Mr. William Acton ?

Acton.   Ay, sir,
And Acton cannot know Colonel Wolfe.

Old A. (coming to Acton, aside). What do you
mean, my son—why this strange anger ?

Acton (to old A.). Do you not see ? Do you not
recognize ? (*Presses his forehead. Wolfe and Barnabas confer aside.*)

Lowe. What the deuce is this ? I surely am not in
the club.

Wolfe (to Lowe). I demand an explanation.

Bar. (to Acton). Yes, sir, you must explain why you
    cannot
Know my friend.

Acton.   For the simple reason that
I know him far too well already.

Wolfe.   Know me ?

Acton. As a villain—a base, consummate villain.
    (*Wolfe furiously grapples with Acton, who flings
    him off. The parties present interfere.*)

Wolfe. Unhand me, Barnabas : shall I submit
To a blow—

Bar.   No ; but this is not the way—

Wolfe. You are right—there must be blood : see
    to it.

Bar. (to Wolfe). Stand back. We must have an
apology, or a meeting. Sir, an ample apology.

Acton. Apology ! To that worthless scoundrel ?
You much mistake me, sir. 'Twould seem, likewise,
You equally mistake your friend. He will
Scarcely demand one when he knows me.

                (*Wolfe tries to distinguish Acton.*)

Lowe. What does all this mean !

Bar.   Who, then, are you, sir ?

Acton. Nay, sir, speak for your friend ; who has I
    deem,

As many aliases as any rogue

Of London.   Let Colonel Wolfe, if such be

In truth his name—

Lowe.   It is his name.

Bar.   Why do you doubt it ?

Acton.   I have known him by

Another—one associated with

The foulest infamy.

Wolfe (*aside*). Ha !

Acton (*looking full at Wolfe*). Look at me, Alfred
    Stevens,

For such I still must call you :—look on me.

Behold one who is ready to avenge

Margaret Cooper's bold and deep betrayal.

Ha ! villain, do you start !   Do you shrink ?

Do you remember the smooth-spoken knave

Who, thus to doubly foul all moral law,

In the staid garment of a preacher sought

The home of innocence to wreck its peace,

And its young inmate ruin.   Once before

We met in strife.   Your hellish purpose then

Had not been consummated.   Would to heaven

I had slain you on the spot.   'Tis not too late

For vengeance.   (*Wolfe recovers his self-possession.*)

Wolfe. The man is mad.   I know not what he means

Acton. Liar ! This will not serve you.   You shall not
    'scape me.

You can't deceive the eye of honesty.

The trembling eddies of your secret soul,

If such dark conscience hath a living soul,
Break on your face and accent, and aloud
Proclaim the wretch I have pronounced you.
 Bar. This is very strange (*aside*).
 Wolfe.   Sheer madness :
Or 'tis a low, political design,
To undermine by an unmanly fraud,
The reputation you can't fairly shake :
A poor, base trick—but let the sland'rer know
The people understand these things too well.
 Acton. They shall know thee better. Alfred Stevens,
The charge I utter you dare not deny.
 Wolfe. It is as false as hell !
 Acton.   'Tis true as heav'n ;
And atonement craves—blood only will suffice.
 Lowe. Dear me! My dear friend, you are a young
  man ;
Perchance you are mistaken : let me beg,
Just for your own sake, you admit so much,—
And shake hands on it.
 Acton.   Sir !
 Bar. I am sorry you persist in this unhappy business.
 Wolfe. Pshaw ! The fellow is a madman or a fool ;
Why trouble yourself further. Let him have
Whate'er he wishes.
 Bar.   My friend will withdraw.
I shall wait on you immediately.
      (Bar. *and* Wolfe *retire up*.)
 Acton. I shall await you (*going*).
 Lowe. My dear friends, I regret—(*to Acton*.)
 Acton (*going*).   No apology :
You have, sir, unintentionally done
The greatest favor you could have conferr'd

Upon me—placing that bad man within
My grasp.

Lowe. I am a most unfortunate man, to be a cause of
bloodshed.

Acton.　　　　　Fortunate rather,
In being even the unknowing means
Of avenging a woman's honor.　　　　[*Exit* ACTON.

Old A. Let me request a pledge of secrecy, Mr. Lowe,
as to what you have witnessed.

Lowe. Certainly, my good sir, I have no desire to
make myself responsible for any thing not belonging to
me.　I'm as secret as the grave.

　　　　　　　　[*Exit* OLD A. *and* MR. LOWE.

Bar. I saw at once the fellow's tale was true.　It was
so like you.

Wolfe. How if I deny it?

Bar. I wouldn't believe you.　Where's the girl now?

Wolfe. That is a mystery I should not mind
Paying to find out.　A splendid creature!

Bar. I reckon this fellow loved her.

Wolfe.　　　　　　　　　He did.
A rude, half-witted sort of rustic he,
At Eaglemont.　Margaret despised him.
'Tis true, we almost fought for her before.
Ashley, if I remember, was his name.
Could I have dreamt, that in him I'd behold
The now quite noted Acton.　Barnabas,
Look you! We did not think the pistol might
Aid us to level our young orator.
Ha! ha!

Bar.　　　And will you do it?

Wolfe. There's no alternative.　He will have none:
And should he blab—

　　　　　　4*

Bar. Wing him ! that will be enough

Wolfe. Curse him ! Who made him Margaret's champion ?

Were he her husband I might let him off
With moderate chastisement, but he must pay
The penalty of upstart insolence.
I owe him an old grudge, too.   He struck me
On that day at Eaglemont.

Bar. He did !

Wolfe. I feel it now.   I will *kill* him.
Ev'n if I had not ground most personal,
Think what a stroke of policy it were
To get him from the field.

Bar. But what if he shoots ?

Wolfe. Ah ! (*thinking*) secure *my* distance, a little
adroitness will give me the advantage.

Bar. And you will commission the bullet—
You will kill him ?

Wolfe. I must.   [*Exeunt.*

Re-enter OLD ACTON *and* WILLIAM ACTON.

Old A. Do not be downcast.   I know not how you
could have acted otherwise ; and yet the affair is very
shocking.

Acton. It is ; but crime is shocking, and so are
The thousand deeds that hourly rack man's life,
Though hourly, death admonishes to good.
Therefore the best philosophy is that
Which girds us up with resolution
To meet what seems as unavoidable,
As though we were prepared for death.

Old A. It *may* be death, my son.

Acton.   And if it were,

And brought a sight of vengeance with it, then
I could feel happy.   When I think of her—
So beautiful, so proud, so bright, so dear
Then to this heart—so dear to me, ev'n now
I feel the worthlessness of my life's laurels.   (*Weeps.*)

 Old A. Give way not thus, my son.   Be a man.

 Acton. Am I not ?   What have I not endured—what
Have I not o'ercome.   Will you not suffer
A little moment's weakness, in exchange
For those dread years' convulsive silence.

 Old A. It is worse than useless to brood, my son,
Upon those days.

 Acton.   What might they not have been.
And now, I see her as an angel fall'n ;
And in this wretch the arch-fiend.   Oh ! surely,
To slay *him* cannot be an endless crime.

Enter BARNABAS.

 Bar. Very awkward business, Mr. Acton—no adjusting it now.   May I have the pleasure of knowing your friend ?   (*Acton bows and hands him a card.*)

 Bar. (*Reads aloud.*) Major Randolph.

 Old A. (*coming forward takes the card from Bar.'s
   hand*). *I* will act for you, William.

 Acton. You, sir ?

 Bar. You, old gentleman ?

 Old A. Yes.   Shall I be more reluctant than you to serve a friend.   This, sir, is my adopted son.   I love him as if he were my own.   I love him better than life. Shall I leave him at the very time his life is perilled ! No, sir.   I am sorry for this affair, but will stand by him to the last.   Let us see to the arrangements.

 Bar. You have seen service before, old gentleman.

Old A. I have been young.

Bar True blue, still.   Though I regret equally with yourself the sad duty, yet it gives me pleasure to deal with a gentleman of the right spirit.   I trust your son is a shot.

Old A. He has nerve and eye.

Bar. Good things enough—very necessary—but a spice of practice does no harm.   Now, Wolfe has a knack with a pistol that makes it *curious* to see him, if you be *only a looker on.*

Old A. Let me stop you, sir.   When I was a young man, such a remark would have been held an impertinent intimidation.

Bar. Egad, you have me !   Are we agreed on the weapons—shall it be pistols ?

Old A. Yes—at sunrise to-morrow.

Bar. Good.

Old A. Place—Red Grange.   Distance—

Bar. Twelve, I suppose—usual thing.

Old A. (*after a momentary pause*).   We will settle that on the ground.

Bar. (*Bites his lip.*)   Well, to-morrow morning— Red Grange—

Old A. At sunrise.

(*Picture.   Barnabas in the doorway.*)

ACT III.

SCENE I.—*Exterior of the Red Heifer Inn.*

Enter MR. LOWE *from Inn.*

Lowe. Bad business, by Jove! and may be a sad business, too. Acton is too wild and Wolfe too wary for good to come of it. So much for my leaving the town, and becoming political mediator in the heat of a raging election. But my conscience is clear as to my good intentions. How could I tell that Wolfe was such a scapegrace, and Acton such a perfect wildcat. I gave sound advice, too, but it was well I was not eaten up alive. I'll make back to town as expeditiously as possible, and if any of these fire-eaters get me in their trail, under any pretence whatsoever, again, my name is not Lafayette Hancock Lowe. Something is done by this, for here comes Barnabas, and alone. What if Wolfe is killed?

Enter BARNABAS.

What news, Barnabas?

Bar. Good news.

Lowe. Is Wolfe killed?

Bar. Would that be good news?

Lowe. Well, there might be worse and there might be better. What is your good news?

Bar. Here it is—　　　　　[*They stand aside.*

Enter OLD ACTON *and* SURGEON *supporting* WILLIAM ACTON, *who is pale and feeble.*

Acton. I am better—the cloud has gone from my

eyes. Forgive me, father, if in this I have gone against your will. I deeply deplore the pain I inflict on you, which I know is more acute than what I feel—forgive me.

Old A. Bless you, my son ; you have acted as became a man. (*With great affection.*) Let us go in.

Surgeon. The sooner he is completely at ease the better. The wound, though not mortal, is of a delicate and perhaps tedious nature.

[*Exit* OLD A., ACTON, *and* SURGEON, *into Inn.*

Lowe. Is that your good news ?

Bar. It is better than I expected to have. But for the old fellow's pluck the young one would have been a dead man.

Lowe. Ha ! How so ?

Bar. Why, at ten paces Wolfe is sudden death ; but Old Acton had the choice of distance, and insisted on five paces, back to back, wheel and fire.

Lowe. Oh, the old blunderbuss—a most murderous affair.

Bar. The suddenness of the proposition rather irritated Wolfe, who counted on ten ; but for that the news might have been much worse.

Lowe. And Wolfe ?

Bar. Had a very narrow escape—Acton's ball took the brim off his hat, just over the ear—he's gone across the country to Clifden's.

Lowe. I'm off in the other direction—to town—after I congratulate my friends.

Bar. If this affair is mentioned, just stop all conjectures on the matter, by alluding to it as a political difference.

Lowe. I assure you I will not make the slightest allu·

sion to it—none at all, whatever. I will not make myself responsible to either party by telling any of their
stories. Just think of my meeting Old Acton, at five
paces, with double-shotted howitzers. No, no—good-
day—adieu.

    [*Exit into Inn. Exit* BARNABAS *opposite side.*

   SCENE II.—*Room in Eustace Clifden's house.*

     CLIFDEN, *seated.*

 Clif. If she could marry, she would marry me :
She will not—cannot—yet she would.
She loves no other : I love her alone—
And yet between us as between two banks
Of some wide stream, the throbbing tide of life
Rolls on, and fretfully on either shore
Splashes fond discord, that in echoes mock
The restless pleadings at the distant side.
Must it be thus ? It cannot. I must solve
The mystery in which she is enwrapped.
To go, a prey to mad conjecture, were
A living death, less torturous only
Than this undying love.
The clouds must part, and I the barrier see
That dims my path, and keeps my sun from me. (*Going.*)

  Enter RUFUS WOLFE, MAUDE, *and* JANETTE.

 Maude. Whither, brother? We have been seeking
  you.
 Clif. (*disconcerted*). Why, my friend, I did not dream
  you were
Within a dozen miles of us.
 Wolfe.   While you

Were rusticating I have been at work ;
And just rode over to confer upon
Our prospects ; but, instead of finding you
In mood for council, strong with healthy wit,
Such as these glorious country scenes inspire,
I meet you moody and weighed down as 'twere
With premonitions of defeat.   Cheer up,
Clifden, the prospect brightens day by day.   .

    Clif. (*musingly*). Indeed.

    Jan. (*mimicking him*). Indeed—why yes—and so
       it is.

(*To Wolfe.*) Ah, Colonel, Love and Politics cannot dwell
With harmony in that frail tenement.
Love is sweet music, full of pettish airs,
And thoughtful pain, and pleasures without thought ;
While Politics is selfishness grown bold,
And for its ends confusing all things else.
Love is the heart, and Politics the head,
And when there's strife between them, I well know
Which side good Cousin Eustace takes.

    Maude. Ah, he has seen his goddess of the Wood—
(*To Clifden, playfully*)—Have you not, brother ?

    Jan.   To be sure he has ;
Naught else could make him look so cheerful.

    Maude. Janette, you vex Eustace.

    Wolfe. I did not dream such sweet allurement 'twas
That held our brilliant Clifden from the town.
Who, may I ask, is she that hath this magic wrought ?

    Maude. Had you but seen her you would wonder not
That he's possess'd with sudden passion for
The air she breathes—indeed, she's beautiful !

    Clif. (*abstractedly*). Very beautiful, Maude !

    Jan. Yes, a thunder-storm sort of beauty ;

A dark and dismal grandeur, that outflashes,
Dazzling and terrifying one's poor heart.

   Clif. Ha ! neither over nor under drawn.

   Jan. To be sure not.   Why, Colonel, when we first
Were left together, I felt crumpled up
With very fear.

   Maude.   Now, cousin, 'tis unkind
To harrow thus the mind of our dear Eustace.
A different likeness of fair Sybil, I
Can show.   True, she is sad, and grave betimes,
And wrapt in volumes that we can but name,
But then she's kind, and from her gloomiest moods
Wakes into gentle radiance, like the moon,
Dispelling doubt that only came when we
Were in the dark.

   Clif. (*aside*) Dear sister !

   Wolfe. Can we not see the fair one? You have roused
My curiosity almost to envy.
Is the fair solitary's grot remote ?

   Jan. About a mile—a tassle as it were
Upon the fringe of the forest.

   Clif.   The lady
Is engaged to-day, and—

   Wolfe.   So am I :
Nor would I mar the sweet seclusion which
Hath the chief eloquence when lovers meet.
But, Clifden, I would speak to you of what
Our merry-hearted friends take little heed.

   Jan. What's that ?

   Wolfe. Myself.

   Jan. Had you said one of us, we both might feel
A cause of quarrel o'er the pleasant doubt :
But as you made our heedlessness all one—

Maude. Why, then, we'll take notes quietly to solve
Whose careless tongue has most distracted
His to such a speech. Ha! ha! Come, cousin,
Come.

    Wolfe. And may I hear the court's decision?

    Jan. If we can decide. Ha! ha!

                [*Exit* MAUDE *and* JANETTE.

    Clif. You will excuse my bluntness, if I pray
That you postpone—

    Wolfe.   I see impatience writ
On every movement, Clifden. I will not
Waste a word ; but, as I leave within the hour,
Would fain impress you with the duty which
We owe—not to ourselves, for that were base
In its selfish ends—but to our country.
We much depend on you : your gift of speech,
Your crowd-controlling phrases, ready wit ;
Your mastery of passion, that great drug
Which gives the secrets of the populace
A flavor of the heart ; and makes each man
Of all the wondering multitude believe
The speaker spoke for him alone ;—with you
To fling these quick'ning seeds broadcast into
The ready hotbed of the people's hearts,
Success is certain. Acton now is powerless.

    Clif. You've never heard him speak, or you would feel
What baseless praises you have heaped on me.

    Wolfe. I have heard him once, and had Fate been
        kind
As she has been, he never would be heard again.

    Clif. I do not understand you—

    Wolfe.   Simply this :
We met last night, and he, in violation

Of even plebeian hospitality,
Hung a base fabrication to my name :
We met this morning, and I shot him.
   Clif. Unfortunate !
Wolfe.   Yes, that I did not kill him.
Clif. Thank heaven, he is not dead !—
Wolfe. He is, however, beyond all usefulness ;
And if you but leave your forest beauty—
Pardon me—for a few days, the game is ours.
   Clif. As I promised, I shall do : but I grieve
This early bloodshed on our side.
   Wolfe.   Pshaw !
All you lovers grow so tame in cooing
Delicate fantasies to maiden ears,
That oft I wonder how the maiden bends
To such unmanly chirpings.
   Clif. (*satirically*).   To-morrow
I shall feel stronger of voice : strong enough,
Mayhap, to drug the crowd, as you infer.
To-day, you see I have a fantasy
Most delicate for other ears.   Adieu !   [*Exit.*
   Wolfe. Touchy and stubborn, as all lovers are ;
Or, as they think they must be unto all
Who will not mount with them the airy stilts
On which they poise unsteady phrases
Of devotion and what not ; all of which
But tempt the exercise of woman's power :
These women, who, like all great victors, live
On the weak homage of their pris'ner's praise.
Who can she be that holds his heart ?   Methinks
Its heat will burn her fingers and exhaust
Itself.   His nature runs into extremes.
Frantic a day—a month melancholy—

An hour's passion, and a season's pain.
His passion's up to-day, but, too ripe fruit,
To-morrow's sun will melt it to the earth.   [*Exit.*

SCENE III.—*A plain, but neatly furnished room in Mrs. Hardy's
          cottage. Book-case, table, &c.*

SYBIL *seated, her head buried in her hands.*

Sybil (*rising*). Why do I weep? Have I not said the
          word
That should dry up these fountains of the eye
Which are the tender emblems of affection !
Tears ! What right have I with tears ? I whose lone
          hope
Feeds on the sparks that iron destiny
Strikes from the heart that's hardened into flint.
O woman ! image of all feebleness
Art thou. These garments are its badges. How long
Must I still crave for retribution ?
A day, an hour would have given to a man
That prompt revenge which I have sought for years.
(*Muses.*) Fool that I was to have denied his suit.
Why did I not, at least, accept his *hand*—
The hand of man ! He is an avenger
Sent from heaven, and I have cast him off.
What is love, life, or fear, or joy to me,
That I should weigh distinctions ?
What is his love to me, that I should fear
To use it for my hate ? He still is mine
If I but say it ; and not to say it,
Is to fling away the weapon heaven sent.
I cannot doubt his love ! His love—ha ! ha ! ha !
Man's love ! that brilliant shroud for infamy.

(*Pauses.*) Eustace Clifden, thou art mine : I take thy
　　hand
And place within it all my woes, my wrongs,
My pent-up, silent-growing rage of years.
I take thy hand as Judith took the sword
That freed her from the libertine.
Oh, how near losing, by a word, was I, 　　•
The means of making vengeance perfect.
Yet while I plan perchance he flies the place,
And leaveth nothing but his heart behind.
I claim his hand—his *hand* is *all* I need.

　　(*Rushes to the door, opens it quickly, and falters
　　　　on the threshold. Her arm drops. She re-
　　　　turns, wearing an expression of remorse.*)

Oh Sybil, Sybil, thou'rt indeed debased.
What ? Would'st thou send to shame, perdition, death,
This youth, whose only crime is loving thee ;
And who, if he had never seen thy face,
Would mount to honor in the face of earth.
What ? Would'st thou fling thine arms about his heart,
And dupe his ardent nature to thy hate
With wanton kisses, weighty in deceit ;
Decoy his soul from out himself, and guage it
To the dim path where moans thy wrathful fate ? 　　•
Oh, no—no—no—I must not wrong him thus :
So young, so generous, so full of truth,
And lovingness, and manly speech.　Away
Ye fiends that wait on woman's doubts, to make
Her less than woman.　(*Falls, weeping.*)

　Enter MRS. HARDY.　*Goes to Sybil and raises her.*

　Mrs. Har. Why, daughter, will you drive yourself into
These paroxysms.　Why waste your strength upon

The arid past, when it is needed for
The present and the future.

Sybil.   The present?
I have no present ; and with such a past,
Can have no future.

Mrs. Har.   Oh, must we ne'er,
Ne'er rid us of that past.   Must you still cry—
Shame, shame, aloud, at thy poor self, now that
You have not the loud world to do it ?   Shame !
The past !   Have you not expiated it ?
Have you not made me suffer for it ?   Oh,
There are other things to live for now.

Sybil.   True,
There are ; and if there were not, then, indeed,
Should I be desperate.

Mrs. Har.   You have, my child,
Much, I hope, to live for yet ; new life of joy :
With our long solitude and altered name
The girl of Eaglemont's forgotten quite.
Ay, you will yet as good a husband have
As any girl in the land.

Sybil.   Oh, mother,
Mother ! for the sake of heaven, none of this.

Mrs. Har. Why not ?   Should brain and beauty, such
        as yours,
Be buried here for ever ?

Sybil.   Peace, mother !
Peace—you will drive me mad.

Mrs. Har.   Well, daughter, well,
I know not how to please you, but I'm sure
I only want to cheer and lift your heart ;
Your hopes are not so bad as you would think—
(*Sybil waves her hand impatiently.*)

No, indeed, not near so bad.　Is there not
Young Clifden fairly dying for your love?
Why will you not wed him?　A better mate
No woman need desire—handsome, young, and good.

　　Sybil. Mother, you have deeply suffer'd for your child—
Torn from the homestead that was sacred made
By my dear father's love—torn from the scenes
Of your bright wedded days—scenes that hold thoughts
Which are the dearest solace of old age,
For in such scenes we live our love anew.
Torn you have been from those tried hearts and eyes
That weave a glory round deserved success ;
You have forsaken every thing to prop
The tottering youth of your once haughty child.
These wrongs, which have upon your waning years,
In their chill weight anticipated age,
Not less than those I've suffer'd, make me quake
To hear you talk as you have done.　Marry?
Clifden——?

　　Mrs. Har. Yes, daughter : think not of my wrongs ·
I cannot long be with you on the earth,
And ere I go 'twould glad my heart to see
You wed to one who in his noble love
Would crown with joy the trials you've endur'd.

　　Sybil. In ev'ry quality of sense and heart
Is Clifden nobly gifted ; but could I
So sacrilegious be as link his fate
And spotless gifts with my unsettled soul !

　　Mrs. Har. If you were married unto such a man,
Your life would have a purpose in his life.
Domestic duties would exalt your mind
Above the wilful dreams of horror, which
You cherish now.　Life would have purpose then.

Sybil. And has it not a purpose now ! A great,
A holy, soul-absorbing purpose.

    Mrs. Har. Daughter, do not look so wild (*puts her
        arm around her*).

    Sybil.   Purpose—
Have I not that oath to fulfil—

    Mrs. Har.   Margaret—
Oh Sybil, dear,—you fright me with these oaths.
What's done cannot be helped. You frighten me.
Be calm—there's some one at the wicket. See,
Clifden's coming up the path.

    Sybil.   I cannot
Meet him. (*Going.*)

    Mrs. Har. For my sake !

    Sybil.   Mother, mother—place
On my affection some more worthy test—
I cannot, cannot marry.

Enter CLIFDEN.

    Mrs. Har. Good day, Mr. Clifden.

    Clif.   Ladies, good day :
Pardon, I pray, this lack of ceremony.
Finding the wicket open, I thus far
Intruded, on a neighbor's privilege,
As to enter—

    Mrs. Har. Your bright face brings its welcome,
The sunshine comes unbidden in, and why
Should you not—

    Clif.   Madam, you are kind, but while
Your daughter's here, there is, I'd say, no need
Of other light.

    Sybil.   Ah, Clifden, you are more
Polite than usual.

Clif.   A just rebuke
For previous want of manners.

Mrs. Har. Sybil is not quite well ; you must not pit
your ready wit against her.   Be seated, Mr. Clifden ; I
will leave you to enliven her, if you are not otherwise
engaged (*Clifden bows*), while I make my domestic
rounds.   (*Sybil exhibits uneasiness and anger at her
mother's leaving.*)   [*Exit* Mrs. Hardy.

Clif. (*approaching*). Miss Hardy—

Sybil (*rising, and raising her hands as if to com-
          mand silence*). Clifden, I supplicate you—
Speak not !   For your own sake and mine do not.

Clif. But—

Sybil (*bitterly*). Why will you, sir, pursue me thus?

Clif. No rest I'll find 'till I the barrier know,
That either in thy self-denying brain,
Or, in the actual fact, divides us.
I love you deeply, passionately !
As I ne'er fancied man could mortal love.
This passion rends my frame, distracts my mind,
And doubtful makes the tenure e'en of life.
I have seen you only to worship you.
Lost to me, I lose my divinities,
My faith.

Sybil. Oh, Clifden, spare *me*, and preserve yourself :
You woo destruction.

Clif.   I can see there is
A deepening mystery about you.

Sybil. Ay, the mystery of a passion which
Controls all others.

Clif.   Then but a pretext
Was your wide, blighting, though deceiving scorn,
For th' all-controlling passion—Love.

Sybil. A pretext? Would it were. Love makes no
part
Of my existence, which now feeds alone
On the heart-hard'ning rival passion—Hate!
   Clif. You hate?
   Sybil.   Ay, sir. Hate is my passion,
And dwells not here alone, since it commands
A slave of its own likeness—
   Clif.   And that?
   Sybil. Is Revenge.
Ask thyself, then, with these within my breast,
Whether there can be room for aught else there.
   Clif. (*pacing to and fro, muttering*). Revenge, Sybil,
      revenge (*stops*)! Something of this
I understand (*cogitates*). Your culture, loveliness,
This solitude. These do not balance well.
(*To her.*) Some ruthless knave, perchance, in usury
      steeped,
Taking advantage of thy mother's weeds,
Thy orphanage, has levell'd all your gods,
Has torn the splendor from your household heav'n,
And revels in the starry wealth once yours,
Mayhap the plunderer would barter it
For that bright beauty he could not enslave.
Your dignity and learning are cramp'd here,
They are not natural to this house or sphere.
You have an enemy—Sybil, I will be
Your greedy champion 'gainst the world. Give me
Your hate, and I will crush what bred it.
   Sybil (*with eager forgetfulness*). Will you indeed do
      this! But what do I say.
No, no—you cannot, must not avenge me.
No, no.

Clif. I will—I can. Your enemy shall be mine—
I will pursue him to the ends of earth.

    Sybil (aside). Sustain me, heaven. (*To C.*) No, no—
        you shall not—
I will not wrong your generosity,
Your daring love, by yielding to your pray'r.
Deeply, sincerely, do I feel for thee—
But (*aside*)—Oh, my brain—my heart will burst (*weeps
        aside*).

    Clif.   Tears !
The words that vainly struggle to the tongue,
Break from the eye in liquid eloquence.
Sybil, I must and shall be your life's shield.
My own heart, in its lack of comfort, prompts
What's due to one, like thine, in agony.
I cannot leave you here alone, a prey
To this revenge, which worketh 'gainst thyself
More than its object, whatsoe'er it be.

    Sybil. You rush upon a fate I'd give my life
To save you from.

    Clif.   Then why not link our lives
Upon it ! It is all I crave.

    Sybil. Heaven is witness how I've striven for you,
And against myself. You seek to fathom
The thoughts that hang like night about my heart.
You love me, Clifden ! I believe you.
You love me, but the secret of my soul
Will be the death-blow to that love.

    Clif. Speak, dearest, speak ! Your anxious fears but
        prove
The tender majesty of woman's soul.
Speak ! I am your bondman.

    Sybil.   But the world's mock—

To see it, in the inner vision, point
Its skinny finger at my tale of woe.

 Clif. Declare my service. Your possession
Will give me deeper purpose on the earth.
You have been wronged, I care not to know more.
My eyes but see you to adore, my ears
But hear your words of virgin purity ;
And in this faith I claim thy hand, thy cause,
Thy wrongs, thy vengeance. Make them mine alone,
That I a bright memorial may raise
Of virtuous revenge, which in the minds
Of men will live when we are in the dust.

 Sybil (aside). How I could love this man. (*Aloud*) I
  beg thee—go.
The fountains of my life are welling up—
My heart, like some weak swimmer, vainly breasts
The tide—it struggles, but it will not save
Itself to risk thy heart a sacrifice.

 Clif. Oh, noblest hearted—let my strength bear thee.
Let our young hearts rest on the other's strength,
And like the 'butments of a bridge, bear up
The single arch of our existence.

 Sybil (abstractedly). What fate is driving me to this
  Can it be
My mind at last has fallen from its throne !
Do I dream ? Oh, Clifden, wilt thou not go—

 Clif. And leave thee victim to thy fantasies,
Or the grim echoes solitude evokes
From old misfortune's crabbed voice ?

 Sybil (looking imploringly to heaven). Give aid, that
  I may drive my heart away ;
For sure no love of man—the man of all I love—
Can stand the ordeal I conjure up.

(*To Clifden*.) The hand you woo was by another won—
Peace—you shall know all.   'Twas in life's early spring.
He found me sparkling in my native hills,
As pure, if wayward, as the young cascades,
That pant to spring out from the yawning glooms.
He found me proudly innocent, and vain
Of girlish triumphs, that not envy's tongue
Could lessen in our happy village.
He reached above my rustic haughtiness
With all the city's legacy of ease,
With bright audacity and subtle force,
With ardor passionately robed in words
Stolen from The Book of Everlasting Love ;
And thus, as 'twere with wizard energy,
My pride, my vanities, my hopes, my life
Of life, under the magic spell-word—marriage—
Were surrounded ; and—

    Clif.   You loved !—ay, love him yet.
(*Sybil goes to the book-case and returns with a pistol.*)
    Sybil. Daily, for five long years, I've practised with
This instrument of death.   Here, in these woods,
I've daily held a calm devotion, where
Hate is the deity and vengeance dark
The officiating votaress.   Love yet !—ha !
For years I've toiled with this delusive dream—
Retribution !   But what can woman do—
Where seek—how find her victim ?   Ah, think you,
Eustace Clifden, could I have met my foe
I would divide the glory of this work
Of gnawing vengeance !—No ! this eye and hand
Are strangers to a woman's fears.

    Clif. (*Taking hold of the hand with pistol*). Give me
    the hand—

                6

Sybil.   Stay—be warned—
Never was man to such conditions brought,
As you to those by which you claim my love.
    Clif. Hear me, thou just, impartial heaven !
To stand between this woman and her wrongs—
To take her heart and shrive it of its hate—
To make her woes my own—
    Sybil.   Do not mock me.
The barrier cannot, must not be o'erstepped.
    Clif. I swear by this fair hand—
    Sybil.   Swear not, and be free :
The hand you clasp is a dishonored hand !
    Clifden (recoils and drops her hand).
    Sybil (with calm passion). Who takes my hand must
        take the weapon from it.
My husband must avenge his wife's dishonor.
    Clif. (clasping her hand). Thy hand, thy hate is mine.
    Sybil. The oath !
    Clif.   I swear !
        (*Sybil, overcome, hysterically falls into Clifden's
        arms.*)

————◆————

ACT IV.

SCENE I.—*Room in Clifden's House.*

EUSTACE CLIFDEN.   RUFUS WOLFE.   BARNABAS.

Wolfe. Truly, Clifden, I congratulate you.
Your wife's a noble woman : and her mind
As richly gifted as her beauty's rare.
    Clif. I'm proud to think my best friends all agree,
I'm right in love as sound in politics.
    Wolfe. Fortunate fellow ! I should say no man
Was ever more so. But your happiness
Will quickly end the reign of bachelors—
They'll want to rival your good fortune.
Shall we not give him a certificate,
On the unusual wisdom of his choice,
Making him free of all Club penalties
Made against those who wed without its leave ?
    Bar. I suppose so, if you say it. I judge
Only of Mistress Clifden's lovely mien,
For you her conversation all engross'd.
I'll certify she's noble to the eye,
And take your measure of her mental worth.
    Wolfe. You will be safe in doing so.
    Clif. My friends, she's noble and as eloquent
Ev'n as she looks. Could I say more—
    Wolfe.   Or less !
    Clif. But come, had we not best be on the road.
    Wolfe. I fear my horse will not carry me. The brute
is snagged, or has a nail in his foot ; the quick is touch-
ed ; and indeed, but for the brute's sake, I'm not sorry.

We roused too late last night, and I have—a slight
headache. I'll nurse myself this morning.

Clif. Shall we break up our excursion, Barnabas?

Bar. No, by Jove! I need fresh air after exhausting
all my breath in taverns for the public good.

Clif. Come, then : make yourself at home (*to Wolfe*),
you will find
Some books about the house.

Wolfe. Thanks, my dear boy!—I feel myself at home.
(*Detains Barnabas.*)

Clif. (*to Bar.*). I shall await you at the stables. [*Exit.*

Bar. What's the matter?

Wolfe. The strangest in the world.
Would you believe it, that girl, about whom
I fought with Acton, and young Clifden's wife,
Are one and the same person!

Bar. (*gives a long whistle*). The devil they are!

Wolfe. True! I have spoken with her as Margaret:
The recognition is complete.

Bar.　　　　　　　　　Heavens!
How awkward.

Wolfe.　　　　Awkward! On the contrary,
This meeting I regard as fortunate,
Most fortunate : I ne'er was satisfied
With having lost her as I did ; and now
To find her, is like finding a rich prize
I thought forever lost.

Bar.　　　　　　　　Do you not fear—
Might she not hint it to her husband?

Wolfe. She's not the fool you show yourself to be.
What wife would do it? or what woman? No—
She kept her secret when she married him,
And will not blab it now.

Bar.   But the affair
With Acton has from Clifden's ears been kept,
Only because he had no ear for aught
Save love.   He soon must hear of it.
    Wolfe. No mischief can it work.   Did you not hear
Me ask him on our last night's rouse the name—
The maiden name of Mistress Clifden.   Ha!
Forsooth the *maiden* name—ha ! ha ! ha !
    Bar. Yes ; her name, he said, was Hardy.
    Wolfe. Sybil Hardy—*his* Sybil !   Ha ! ha ! ha !
    Bar. Do not laugh so loud—
    Wolfe.   You are as timid
As a hare in December.   Don't you see
She has imposed upon him a false name.
What matters it to him, then, should he hear
Of Margaret Cooper and myself from this
Till doomsday.   Clifden's safe in ignorance,
As in its knowledge are his wife and I.
At the same time, however, 'twill seem well
You give him true account of Acton's brawl—
All politics, all politics—you know :
High words, and, to sum up the argument,
When reason failed and passion was supreme,
Exchange of shots, and so forth—do you see?
    Bar. That may be very well—but, Jupiter !
I'd rather we were safely from this house.
Yes, yes—I will be off to-morrow.
    Wolfe. Then, by Venus ! you will start alone
Having beheld her, I'm convulsed with joy !
I see her now !
Those wild, bright, almost fierce, dilating eyes ;
Those lips, that brow, that full and heaving breast—
    Bar. Hush, you are mad.   You say you spoke with her :
                        6*

And did she calmly listen, nor abuse
Your wild audacity.

Wolfe. Pah ! Simpleton,
You ne'er could understand her. You must not
Think of this glorious creature as you would
Of ordinary and weak-soul'd women.
Abuse ? She is too proudly built for that—
She threatened me. Ha ! ha ! ha !

Bar. And you—

Wolfe. I laughed, of course ; and but your cursed return
With her boy-husband baulked me, should have met,
And silenced her brave threats with kisses.

Bar. You'll have your throat cut one day or other
By some husband.

Wolfe. Ah ! Barnabas, you know
Little of husbands as you do of wives.
But in her love I've good security ;
Better even than in your stupidity.

Bar. Take care !

Wolfe. She loves me—

Bar. The deuce she does !
You're a conceited fellow.

Wolfe. I know she does.
The strongest passion is youth's mem'ried love :
Its freshness, bloom, and fragrance, never fades.
Think you a woman like her can forget
The lips that first within her bosom blew
The spark of love into a passionate flame ?

Bar. Under the circumstances, she'd be less
Than woman if she could forget you ; but
She seems so proud and cold : at times almost
So fiendish, I should not care to jog
Her memory about such days.

Wolfe. Masks, glorious masks—indignant virtue, ha!
Now, in the morning neither of us leave.
Fortune favors me—you'll not be less kind.
You to my aid must come, good Barnabas.
　　Bar. What? to carry off our hostess ! May I be—
　　Wolfe. Don't—indeed, you will.
　　Bar.　　　　　　　　　To have that fellow,
Who is a perfect Mohawk when aroused—
What ? Clifden in my war-path—on *my* trail—
To slit my carotid—not I—never.
　　Wolfe. I say there is no cause of fear to you :
Keep out of sight, by keeping him away.
You wish to ramble, I do not.　He knows
I've no great relish for horse-exercise.
For you he'll start an elk-hunt, any thing :
To go, I naturally will decline ;
And if you both could only break your necks,
It would be all the better.　She won't miss
Either of you, I'll wager on't.　Ha ! ha ! ha !
But, seriously, you're not in danger's way.
I'm the offender—if offence there be ;
And surely, you'll oblige a friend.
　　Bar.　　　　　　　I don't
Half like such test of friendship.
　　Wolfe.　　　　　　　Paltry test—
There was a time you would not e'en have dared
To refuse me.
　　Bar.　　　Ahem—Clifden awaits me (*going*).
　　Wolfe. Remember, while you're in his company
Keep out of mine and Margaret's.
Pleasant sport to you.　Adieu !
　　　　　　　　　　　[*Exit at opposite sides.*

SCENE II.—*Another room in Clifden's house.*

SYBIL HARDY.   MAUDE.   JANETTE.

Maude. Why sad, sister Sybil? But three days ago and you were so bright and lively, that even Cousin Janette was dull in comparison.

Jan. Heigho! Eustace is away, and young wives are jealous of the magnets that draw husbands from their eyes; but, pet, he will be back soon. He is tearing over the hills, thinking only of his enjoyment. Ha! ha! Heigho! *I* never will get married if I am to feel as you do.

Sybil. You never will feel as I do.

Jan. What—have you a monopoly of affection?

Maude. Do not mind the teaze. Cousin can return to mother, and I will stay with you.

Sybil. Dear Maude, I will be well presently. I am so unused to society—I live and love so much in solitude—my household is so simple, that the very attention due to our guests has excited me more than one might dream of.

Jan. Ah, ha! Maude. Our lovers love to be alone. You could not comfort her more than by leaving.

Maude. But Eustace's sister—

Jan. Is a poor apology for Eustace himself. Come, child, come. (*To Sybil.*) Am I not, Sybil, the best comforter. (*Sybil smiles.*) Ah, I knew it. See that telltale smile. Come, Maude.

Maude. I have a great mind to stay. But—

Jan. Come, coz, come. (*Maude going, but returns and kisses Sybil.*)   [*Exit* MAUDE *and* JAN.

Sybil (*after a pause*). Oh, what a fate this thirsting for revenge

Has brought upon us, Eustace.   Bitterly
I feel my utter degradation.
But I was mad.   When I swore thee, Clifden,
To slay this wretch, the woman I was not
That now I am.   I did not know how much
I loved thee ; or what love thy love begot.
The secret I must keep—this bloodshed stop :
My husband's life is dearer than revenge.
Oh, had the years since last I saw this fiend
Been filled with prayers of penitence, not pride ;
Prayers for grace from heav'n, not for hate on earth,
Thy hand (*kneels*), great Father, were less heavy now.
Spare me, spare me ! Let the trial be light.
Oh, grant thy mercy on my husband's head,
And give me strength, composure, and resolve,
To meet this issue, as it must be met,
Once and forever. (*Starts to her feet as she hears a noise.*)

Enter RUFUS WOLFE.

Wolfe (*approaching with eagerness*). Oh, for this
        meeting how I've wept and pray'd—
With one so loved, so dearly loved—so long
And bitterly lamented.   Margaret—
    Sybil. Sir, you see the wife of Eustace Clifden.
    Wolfe. It is my sad misfortune that you are
His wife, or wife of any heart but mine.
Turn not away—you think I have wrong'd you.
    Sybil. Think, sir, *think*—it matters little unto you
What I may think.   Remember you're a guest
Beneath my husband's roof.   Remember, too,
Thy life is forfeit, as thy love was sworn
To me and mine ;—that in his ignorance

Of your black crime, your safety only lies.
One word from me—

    Wolfe.   You will not speak that word.

Margaret—

    Sybil (with satiric scorn). Will I not !

    Wolfe. For the sake of the dear past you will not.

    Sybil. The past ! Ah, were the past alone my guide,
I should not for my vengeance think of *him.*
An injured woman has a twofold strength.
Proud in the memory that she once was pure,
She holds the woman's nature still ; besides
The fallen angel that informs her hate,
A never absent Lucifer : both strong
To nerve the arm and unsex the brain,
If the dread past alone did beckon me.

    Wolfe. If you the cruel necessity but knew
That kept me from you.

    Sybil. Oh, false, false—and not more false than foolish.
I heard all—I know all. I know that I
The credulous victim of your subtle arts
Have been ; and you, successful coward, boasted
Over the conquest of a trustful girl.

    Wolfe. The villain lied who told you this.

    Sybil. Then, your own acts that lying villain prove.
If you were true, you had no need to shroud
Your purposes within a name as false.
Why fly? Why not have kept the word to which
I fell a sacrifice ? Why for long years
Leave me the miserable mock of those
Who once were even proud of my contempt—
Living, desperately weak, insanely sane,
Verging on madness, that from day to day
Kept in my hand an instant means of death,

Which I did only not use on myself,
In the wild hope that I should meet with you.
  Wolfe. I am here now. If needful be my death
To your sweet peace, command it, in love's name.
  Sybil. A month ago I needed no such offer—
That time has changed me. Nature has succumbed
To the great bliss of being truly loved.
Go—live ! Let not the morrow find you here :
Forget that you have ever known me ;
Forget, if possible, you Clifden know,
For whose dear sake, alone, I spare you. Go ! (*Moves.*)
  Wolfe. For *his* sake, Margaret (*smiling*)—his sake !
      No, no (*offers to take her hand*)—
It is impossible this young man could
Fill up the radiant hopes of such a soul,
Or any thing to such a woman be,
As you, who must remember that first love—
  Sybil. Man or devil, remind me not of crime
That still demands my sworn vengeance.
Hark ye, Alfred Stevens (*almost in a whisper*), you are
      not wise—
You are in the very den of danger.
I tell thee, Stevens, that I spare your life,
Though the weapon is shotted ; though the knife
Is whetted. I spare you, even though I feel
The thirst to slay you rising in my soul,
On one condition—that you do depart.
Wake not my slumbering fury. Linger
Longer, and you may ne'er depart again.
  Wolfe. Why, this is madness.
  Sybil.   I am mad !
And otherwise than mad I cannot be
While you are here.

Wolfe. I cannot think you hate me.

Sybil. Can I think *you* ever loved me ? No, no.
Do not deceive yourself (*Wolfe looks fawningly at
    Sybil*) ; provoke me not
With your defiling glances, and still less
With your dishonest tongue. Be warned in time ;
Another day, and the command I hold
Upon myself, may die through sheer excess
Of agony that keeps it strong to-day.
To destroy you would gratify the hate
I've lived for, but 'twould also overthrow
The peace of *him* I prize beyond my life.
I strive not 'gainst my vows, in your behalf ;
Not e'en in my own behalf the effort springs :
It is for him, who gave me love, new life,
A holy purpose with that name of names—
That name which, truly worn, is the richest gem
All earth can place on woman—name of wife.
It is for him alone, from out whose brain
I have regrown—for my husband, Clifden,
That I avert my vision from the past.
Beware—he comes ! (*Sybil takes a seat at table. Wolfe,
    snatching a book, reclines in an arm-chair, apart
    from her.*)

Wolfe (*rather loudly*). My dear madam, you are right ;
I wonder not you have a preference
For country life : such scenery around,
Such air, the body to invigorate,
Such books to bring the mind perennial strength ;
And, above all, with a companion such
As Clifden, my young, noble friend. Indeed,
I know not which to most congratulate,
You each have made such admirable choice.

Sybil (aside). Villain !

Enter CLIFDEN.

Wolfe. I perceive, madam, by these underscorings, you
are an appreciative student of the great moralist and
man.   Ah ! Clifden, so soon returned, or is it that the
time sped quicker than I thought ?

Clif. Your doubt informs me you were not dull in
my absence.

Wolfe. Oh, not at all, thanks to Mrs. Clifden.   I
took your advice, my dear boy, and made myself quite
at home.   Did I not, my dear madam?   The sight of
these books reminded me of home.   We have discussed
the poets and all kinds of poetry, from the *Paradise
Lost* to the *Loves of the Angels.*   (*Sybil expresses surprise, disgust, and scorn, during this speech.*)

Clif. And which have you decided for ?

Wolfe. Well, strange to say, Mrs. Clifden thinks
Paradise Regained preferable to either, which, you are
aware, is opposed to all critical opinion.

Sybil (aside). Audacious villain !

Clif. (evidently uneasy). Well, you know ladies will
differ with critics ; but you must have talked faster than
we galloped, to get over so much ground in the space of
time.

Wolfe. Then I was right—you hurried back.   Ha !
you rogue, I thought you would not extend your excursion.   Ha! ha ! I was a young married man once myself.

Sybil (to Clif.). You are with us for the evening,
dear ?

Clif. Not yet, Sybil.   Our friend Barnabas is dull to-
day, and dumb.   I strove in vain to rouse him.   Two
miles I jogged beside him for a word—

7

Wolfe. The timid blockhead (*aside*).

Clif. And then bethought me I'd return, run over to Cottageville, bring back Maude and Janette, and thus do all our country life affords to make our city friends in pleasant humor. Here comes dull Barnabas—

Enter BARNABAS.

Bar. At your service.

Sybil. I'll strive and wear his dullness off till you return.

Clif. That were a difficult task, Sybil.

Wolfe. Not so to an enchantress—see her effect on me. You are not jealous, Clifden?

Sybil. Clifden has no need to be.

Clif. Ha! ha! Colonel, you had best take care how you break the wand of your enchantress. Come, Barnabas.

Sybil. Perhaps, Eustace, Mr. Barnabas would rather keep us company—he is tired ; are you not (*to Bar.*) ? You have failed to cheer him (*to Clif.*)—let us try. (*Wolfe motions to Barnabas, unobserved.*)

Bar. I fear, madam, I could ill sustain the gallant Colonel's banter.

Wolfe. Well, with permission of good madam, I will accompany Clifden (*moving*), and you shall discuss the poets.

Clif. Ah, ha! If so, instead of one dull person now, we'd have two on our return. No, Barnabas shall come with me (*exit Sybil*) ; Maude and our witty Janette will teaze him into gay humor on the way back, and then we'll all be ready for a pleasant evening. Is not that best, Sybil (*looks round*) ?

Wolfe. Your wife has an excellently organized mind,

very fine—original and well informed, and gentle too, but a little melancholy, I should say—I will strive to entertain her in your absence.

Clif. Do, Colonel, do. Nothing so pleases her as the dear old books, and talks about them.

Wolfe. Had I your eloquence—

Clif. You are determined to be complimentary. (*To Bar.*) I will wait on you in a moment.   [*Exit.*

Wolfe. How near ruining all my hopes you were, by your infernal dullness.

Bar. I tell you, Wolfe, this recklessness won't do. It is tempting fortune too far. Besides, you owe your election chiefly to Clifden. If he was idle before he married, he certainly exerted himself greatly in your cause since.

Wolfe. How can I repay him better than by conferring all my love upon his wife. I'll get him a good office, too, in the State. You are a dolt. Hear me—take care that you do not betray me by your fears. Could you not get sick at the cottage, and delay, or maybe stay all night, and need his assistance, eh? Do any thing—but keep him out of my way.

Re-enter CLIFDEN.

Clif. Come, Barnabas.

Wolfe. He feels already much better at the prospect of flirting with the girls. He is a great rogue, this Barnabas.

Clif. I must see that he does not steal both their hearts at once.   [*Exit* CLIF. *and* BAR.

Wolfe (*seating himself*). The game goes well. A woman fallen once
Has no retreat. She was mine. She must be mine;

A breath can drive her from her husband's arms.
Little he recks how she once worshipped me—
More wildly e'en than he now worships her.
Little he dreams the secrets that oppress
The pillow next his own.　Little he knows
The bosom that he presses, such adepts
In smiles and strategy these women are.
She comes—with passion for her fear's defence,
But when threats end beseechings will commence.
She's here (*rises to receive her*).

Enter SYBIL.

Sybil (*repulsing him*). Colonel Wolfe, I come to
　　　　warn you once more ;
Again to implore you, leave this dwelling.
You are trifling with your fate !
Wolfe.　　　　　　　　　　Not trifling :
Say it not, my Margaret, *you* are my fate ;
But after such a painful separation
Your greeting's cruel and unnatural.
Sybil. I *am* your fate.　That is the only truth
You utter.
Wolfe.　　Why should recrimination
Coldly invade the precious present.
For the past let my unceasing love atone.
If you e'er loved me as you said you did,
With all the burning fervor of your soul,
Hear me—
Sybil.　　I have no wish to let you add
A second perjury to the first.
Wolfe. It is not perjury : you must hear me
In justification.
Sybil. Justify yourself to heaven, not to me :

I will not hear you doubly curse your soul.
If you have yet a spark of manhood left,
The boon I ask has claims upon you now.
Having trampled me to the dust in shame,
Robbed my bright youth of pride and blissful peace,
Why should you persecute the homely joys
My broken life requires?

    Wolfe.   Persecution?
It is love! You were my first love; you shall be
My last.   We were destined for each other.

    Sybil. Peace! I'm no longer blind and vain as when
My ears were flattered to dishonor.

    Wolfe. Oh that the tongue, whose power you still ad-
      mit,
Could plead its truth to that same ear that once
Delighted in its love.   If you have grown
Insensible to admiration,
Your nature ne'er can grow insensible
To love.

    Sybil. Love—*your* love!

    Wolfe. Yes, Margaret, *my* love.   It conjures up
Moments that were too precious to forget.
Where'er I've been, the memory of that time
Was with me.   'Tis impossible that you,
So full of wealthy nature, and who shared
With me your bosom's first emotions,
Can be so cold.   Your tongue's hot passion proves
The struggle in your heart for its old love—
The sweeping down the trammels of the new.
Do I not know the duties, my beloved,
This new-linked chain imposes?   Have no fear
My sudden joy grim prudence will offend.
No, dearest, no, that self-same prudence will
             7*

Weave round our lovingness a secret bliss,
Which made the gods of old immortal.   Ay,
The kiss that is not trammelled by men's laws
Hath a wild power no legal banns can grant.
Let us, dear Margaret, as when first we loved,
Feed on the stolen rapture of two hearts (*attempts to
        embrace her—she repulses him*).
    Sybil. I have heard you, hellish fiend, to the close :
Oh, would to heaven you had declared yourself
Five years ago as now.   Could I have seen,
As now I see, the cloven foot, the tongue
Of serpent, I had been as pure as you
Were base ; nor would my palsied ear confront
These words accursed—this blasphemy 'gainst God
And man.
    Wolfe. Margaret—
    Sybil.   Sir, I have heard you patiently.   Once
        more—
I hate you with the bitterest loathing ;
With scorn, behold you as the foulest fruit
Hell could bear in black contrast to heaven ;
Whose depth of blackness thwarts the daring scope
Of your atrocious schemes ; abhor you
As a coward below contempt—traitor
To your own sex, and infidel to mine.
Judge, then, the prospect you pursue.
    Wolfe. Beware ! Margaret, beware, lest you rouse
The unearthly terror that you picture.
'Tis you that trifle with your fate.   Despise
My love—you cannot fly my power.
    Sybil. Your power ? Do I rightly hear—Power ?
    Wolfe. Ay, my power : but I entreat you, believe me
your friend.

Sybil. You are my enemy—my first, my worst ;
Heaven forbid that I could think you friend again.

Wolfe. Yet still I am.   I love you better far
Than I have ever loved a woman.

Sybil. You have a wife, Rufus Wolfe?

Wolfe. Yes ; but—

Sybil. And children?

Wolfe. Well—

Sybil. For their sakes if not for mine—for her sake,
Whose dreams are bless'd because she b'lieves you true ;
For the pure babes, who're fed to health or woe
By her sweet peace of mind they mother call :
For their sakes, I implore you to forbear.

> (*Wolfe seizes Sybil ; she escapes, and catching up a
> pistol from the bookcase, turns quickly round and
> presents it at him, just as he reaches within arm's
> length of her : pause and picture.*)

Go (*faltering, her arm drops to her side*)—go ! I spare
       you for the sake of that
Wife and mother you would disgrace.   Go, go—
For you 'tis well that I remembered her.

Wolfe (*aside*). To be thus baited by a frantic woman.
(*Aloud.*) Margaret, this mockery must end.   You talk
Of fear, of fate, of honor, and forget
The greater theme of apprehension, which
To a woman, wife,—and most of all to *you*—
Your husband—

Sybil.   What of my husband?

Wolfe.   Take care—
A word from me, and where is all your peace !
Ha ! am I understood?   Do you not feel
That I have power with one word to give
That living death a proud soul most abhors.

Sybil. Oh, worthy thought, with baseness all com-
    plete,
What a brave treachery, *my friend!*
  Wolfe. Nay, I do not threaten, but remind.
  Sybil. Oh, you are moderate—very moderate!
But know, that ere I wedded Eustace Clifden
I told the shame of this poor hand he wooed.
  Wolfe. You did not—could not—dare not!
  Sybil.   By Him who knows
The secrets of all hearts, I did; nor held
Aught from him, save the name, the public name
As now it doth appear, of my deceiver.
  Wolfe. He would not have married you!
  Sybil. He did, and yet before he did, he swore
On Alfred Stevens to avenge my shame.
'Twas the condition of my hand, dowry,
Fortune, all I brought him—ay, it is true!
  Wolfe. Ha! ha! this tale lacks probability.
I am a lawyer, Margaret, and detect
Its inconsistencies. (*Noise without.*)
  Sybil. They have returned.
Hear me—you're doomed, unless you leave at once.
  Wolfe. I am no child—(*aside*) and you a woman
    are.
  Sybil. Your blood, then, be on your own head. (*Sits
    at table and conceals the pistol in her dress.*)
  Wolfe (*seating himself*). Nothing by assault to be
    done here; however,
Doom, or no doom, to be affrighted I
Am not, fair Mistress Clifden (*aside*).

  Enter CLIFDEN, BARNABAS, MAUDE, *and* JANETTE.

  Wolfe. A welcome back. Good day, ladies, I hope

you have frightened Mr. Barnabas into something like pleasantry.

Jan. Oh, yes, he's merry as a sexton during healthy weather.

Clif. I fear he'll need that functionary soon.
What think you, Sybil ; pining for his Club,
And vowing to be gone ere morrow's noon.

Wolfe. What a compliment to our fair hostess.

Maude and Janette. Oh, Mr. Barnabas !

Bar. Really, ladies, two days out of town undoes my constitution. The country is well enough for a day or so, but—excuse me, ladies—to one like me it is a—a—a bore. Yes, really, I must be off to-morrow.

Wolfe. To morrow ! Will you not wait for me ?

Clif. Of course he will—(*Sybil watching with great anxiety.*)

Bar. How long?

Wolfe. I intended to have stayed but a day or two ; but, bless me, it is so refreshing after our late excitement—besides, the pleasant nature of the topics (*to Sybil*) we have been discussing—that I am induced to make a week of it with Clifden.

Maude and Janette. Bravo, Colonel !

Sybil (*with calm energy*). Colonel Wolfe, that cannot
　　　be. It is
Needful you keep unto your first resolve—
At once. No longer can my husband be
Your host, or in this dwelling wish you grace. (*Astonishment of all.*)

Clif. How, Mistress Clifden ! What does this mean—
to my friend, Sybil ?

Sybil. He is not your friend,

Clifden, nor thine or mine : but let me pass—
I cannot speak here. (*Rushes out.*)

    Clif. Sybil? (*Exit after her.*)

            [*Exit Maude and Janette in consternation*

    Bar. What's this, in the devil's name ?

    Wolfe. In your name, coward.   Can you not see it ?
Have you any weapons ?

    Bar. My pistols are in the saddle-bags.

    Wolfe. Curse the woman—who could have believed it !
Barnabas, should it come unto the worst,
We can but fly.   Look you to the horses,
While I my coolness keep.

    Bar. You wouldn't take my advice ; if—

    Wolfe. This is no time for lecturing.
Your wisdom's always at the eleventh hour.
Your base ingratitude 'tis brings all this.
But hence, if thou would'st not o'erpower'd be,
And slain remorseless in the trap you've made ;
Prepare thyself in haste.   See to the steeds—
If she explain, our start can't be too quick.

               [*Exit hurriedly.*

Re-enter CLIFDEN, SYBIL *clinging to him, both having
hold of the pistol.*

    Sybil. The wrong is mine.   Oh, go not, Eustace,
My hand shall avenge it.   I am sworn to it.
If still the victim, let me victor be.
Your life is precious to me, husband dear,
More precious than the past—or hope, or name.

    Clif. No, Sybil, you are mine, your wrongs are mine :
Before just heaven I renew my oath.

    Sybil. Leave me to shame, despair, to any thing ;
But, Eustace, for the love you bear me, hear ;

For the dear sake of that new-born blessing
Your love has given my nature, hear me.
In the name of every tie that heaven
Welds in the undistinguishable flames
That leap from mutually enkindled souls—
In the name of all such union can inspire,
I here revoke the oath.   When I proposed it
I was not thy wife, but a mad, heartless,
Vengeance-seeking slave.   Nor wife, nor woman
Was I, but am both through thee, and as both,
Revoke that withering and peace-crushing oath.

Clif. Sybil, you're my life : but though you and I
Could in the narrowest corner of the earth
Find untold regions for our happy love,
All land and sea, the huge round globe itself
Hath not extent and verge enough to hold
Thy husband's hand and thy betrayer's heart
Together on it.   While he's upon it
Earth's too confined for me.   While he doth breathe,
I suffocate ; ay, though I stood upon
The healthy heights o' the Alleghanies,
And he on Himalaya's frozen roof,
With toiling nations and big seas between.
While his heart beats, congestion crushes mine.
I must have air.   Which may usurp the earth ?
Either must perish that the other live.

Sybil. Oh, husband.

Clif.   It must be so ; but, Sybil,
Whatever happens, to the last thou'rt mine. (*Kisses her
    and dashes out.*)

Sybil. Thine, Clifden, thine—only thine, ever thine—
To the last—the last—the last. (*Pause, Sybil looks
    about, screams.*)

He is gone, gone—gone for what?
Ha! I have sent him on this bloody work.
Surely it is a madness that doth move me.
Why should he slay Alfred Stevens? Why? (*Presses
        her head.*)
What good will come of it? What safety? What?
(*Pause*) But why should he not! Miserable fate.
Are we never to be free? Must he e'er
Thrust his fiend's visage in our happy homes;
And blast our hopes, our peace, our love for ever?
No, no—ha! ha! ha! Better he should die!
Better we should all die. Strike him, Clifden—
Strike, and fear nothing! Strike for dear virtue
And immortal love! Husband, strike deep—
Strike to the very heart! Strike! Strike! Strike!
                        (*Falls overcome.*)

ACT V.

SCENE I.—*Dungeon.*

CLIFDEN. SYBIL. MR. LOWE.

Sybil. There can be no cause for fear—I have none.
You did not strike for me alone.   The wives,
The mothers, daughters of the State, are all
Your debtors for the deed.   And who that bears
The lordly title, man, will honor risk
To slay a brother for defending woman?
No, I fear not.   If law o'er justice vaunts
I'll go myself into the open court,
And, as 'fore heaven, will the story tell,
In all its plain and foul deformity;
No fear, no shame, shall pale or tinge my cheek,
Or wither, by a fluctuating doubt,
The fact's full force upon the jury's ear.
They *must* believe me when they hear.
    Clif.   My life—
It cannot be.
    Lowe. Will you not be persuaded, my good sir, even
now, at almost the last day, to employ the services of
Acton?   Young though he be, he's skilled, as well you
know, in law; has no superior with a jury, is popular,
and strange to say, likewise pure.   Let me entreat—
    Clif. Did you not say last night he fought with Wolfe
On my account?   What was't?   My senses grow
Dull as these granite walls.
    Lowe. It is well known they quarrelled and fought at
their first meeting, upon political grounds 'twas given
out—

Clif. Yes, I remember—I heard that from Barnabas.

Lowe. But Barnabas, who was present, told me they quarrelled on account of Mrs. Clifden (*looking round*), whose name he said was Margaret.

Clif. Mrs. Clifden! (*Sybil looks up. Clifden motions her to retire. Exit Sybil.*)

Lowe. Pardon me, my young friend, I did not mean to hurt your feelings ; but—

Clif. It was some natural lie of Wolfe's.
It could not be.   Some foul invention
To aid his black designs.   I never heard
Of Acton from my wife.

Lowe. A rumor is abroad which seems to back the assertion. (*Clifden listens eagerly.*) However, whether true or not, Acton must be the man for your defence. Wolfe's friends are very powerful, and will strain every nerve to effect your ruin.

Clif. Well, let them triumph ; they but mimic me :
I've had *my* triumph.   Of a truth, I feel
That I have done the great deed of my life.
Death to me now brings no such agony
As it would bring had I not done this deed.
And yet—to live for Sybil's sake ?   Oh heart !
The thought of losing *her* brings many deaths,
With deeper pangs than the mere loss of life.

Lowe. Allow me to see Acton.

Clif. (*eagerly*). Should I defend myself? Declare the act
And justify it ? (*Pause.*) No : to my own soul—
To God 'tis justified ; but men who judge,
Must know my secret ere 'tis so to them.
The damnèd tale of Sybil's overthrow,
The serpent progress of the venomous head

I've crushed forever, they must hear.   How—how
Can *I* tell *that?*   It is impossible.

   Lowe. If you do not decide quickly your friends must
act for you.   Be advised now—do, Clifden, do.   His
friends *must* act for him (*aside, and going*).

   Clif. I thank you sincerely, indeed I do.
I will think of what you say.   I will—I will. [*Exit* LOWE.

Re-enter SYBIL.

Sybil (*she comes to him and puts her arm about him*),
You never told me your acquaintance with Acton.

   Sybil. Acton—

   Clif. Whom we defeated.

   Sybil. Dear, I know him not.   Let me see—Acton?
'Tis like a waif from my dream-haunted youth.
(*Thinks*) I once did know a person of that name—
An old man—schoolmaster at Eaglemont ;
I have nor seen nor heard of him for years.

   Clif. An old man—how old?

   Sybil. Some five-and-sixty years.

   Clif. It is not the same.   Perhaps he had a son?

   Sybil. He had no son : was never married.

   Clif. It is strange.

   Sybil. What, Eustace—what is strange?

   Clif. Nothing,—nothing.

   Sybil (*aside*). I fear he wanders.   (*He gazes fondly on
and kisses her.*)   Eustace, will you not
Advised be, and give your holy cause
To Acton's hands ?   To him your friends all point
As one above the jealousies that rise
In selfish minds from zeal-distempered politics.
I've heard *you* laud his talents to the skies.

Clif. I have.　All true! but, Sybil, my blood chills
To think of making a defence.

Sybil. Why this strange callousness.

Clif. I killed him ; and evasion would not seek
From the confronted dangers of an act
Deliberate ; and one I'd do again.
Evasion or suggestion cannot come
From me, or any interested in me.
It must not come.　Truth will condemn me, and
I knew it with the weapon in my grasp.

Sybil. What—the *whole* truth condemn us ?

Clif. Perhaps not ; but how to get the whole truth
　　out :
And if it could be done, *I* could not do it.

Sybil. Why not, my husband ?　Shame now's gone
　　from us ;
We are above the world or beneath it.
It gives our hearts no sustenance.　It may
Scorn me, the miserable victim of its ways,
But can it, dare it, call me harlot ?　No !
I did not plunge, but fell into the gulf—
Fell through vain weakness which relied on man :
And, oh, if spirit ever felt remorse
That doth denote wronged virtue's penitence,
Believe me, Clifden, it was mine.

Clif. Do I not know it, dearest (*fondling her*) !

Sybil. I believe you feel it, which conviction gives
Strength to my soul to face a world.　Let it
Know all, if all will any thing avail.
With my own tongue would I declare the facts
Before I'd see thee dragged unto the gallows.

Clif. And I would mount the scaffold a thousand
　　times,

Had I a thousand lives, than suffer you
To work such cruel wrong against thyself.
Live, dearest, live ; and living, daily read
The boast I carve upon my tomb—I died
For thee !　I wed thee for that purpose :
I am true to it.

  Sybil. You said you loved me !

  Clif. And do I not ?

  Sybil.   Eustace, the more one loves
The more he loves to live.　'Tis easier
To die than live ; which makes life beautiful
And grand to those who love ; for love's true tests
Are not so much in overmast'ring hearts,
As that grim world which makes the bright heart black.
Let us o'ercome this world with the truth !
It may frown, but that will only roughen
Its own face, and never ruffle ours.

  Clif. You make me chide myself.

  Sybil. Have we no resource but sorrow, husband ?
Who will meet these judges if not you or I ?
Your friends all point to Acton—why delay ?
Oh, Clifden, husband, let no coward shame
Hide from all ears the tale of your brave blow.
If you or I can't speak, let us heap up
Our two hearts' histories on Acton's soul,
Until he, heated with the treble fires
Of wrong, death, eloquence,—hate, love, and fame,
Shall drive the doubtful demon from men's hearts,
And make them strong for deeds of mercy.
They say he's brave, well-versed, high-minded, pure—
Your lesser self !—What would you more ?

  Clif. No more may be expected of a man.
But wait, wife—wait—to-morrow—

Sybil.   To-morrow !
(*Aside.*) To-morrow, and the chance is lost ; yet I
Stand here as though unwed to my avenger,
Seeing him fade before my very eyes,
Dragging love, life, all hopes of earth and heaven
With him.   I'll see this Acton.   (*Takes a basket and is*
        going—looks at Clifden—returns.
Kiss me, Eustace (*kisses*).   Be cheerful as the day
That saw us wedded (*going*).   'Twas for life *and* death.
                [*Exit, Clifden looking fondly after her.*

SCENE II.—*Room in Acton's house.*

Enter OLD ACTON *and* WILLIAM ACTON.

Acton. How little could I think that Clifden, he
To whom I owe so much of my defeat,
Was married to this girl.   What a wild fate
At once has prompted and waylaid her life—
More wretched ev'n in her triumphal hour
Of vengeance, than in all her days of shame.
    Old A. As dreadful, too, the retribution on
Alfred Stevens.   Little could you have thought
Your boyhood's rival for the village girl
Would be your victor on the wider field
Of politics : Or that his fastest friend
And ablest advocate, in slaying him,
Would by the blow avenge thy youthful wrongs.
This woman's mission has been one of woe ;
My son, 'twas well ye parted in your youth.
    Acton. Had she been mine, this dreadfulest of tales
Would never chill men's veins.
    Old A.   It is a tale
Which future mothers will rehearse, to teach

The heads, if not to touch the hearts, of proud
And wilful daughters.

  Acton.   Can we not aid them?
Clifden's devotion, if not Margaret's wrongs,
Should fire with eloquence some honest voice.
Can we not aid them, father?

  Old A.   How, my son?
Clifden hath all resources of the law;
He hath, besides, a worthy pride of brain.
Our interference might be misconstrued,
If not by him, at least by tetchy friends,
So high the flame of party spirit runs,
As an assumption of superior skill:
And then your duel for the woman's sake,
When her identity is fully known,
Perhaps might only, 'stead of mercy, build
In the censorious such conjecture as
Would act against her.

  Acton. I loved her—she refused me. That is all.—
Is easily told; and I am not the man,
Nor you to teach me, to allow my pride
Rise in rebellion 'gainst a mortal's life.
I loved her—she refused me. (*Muses—turns aside and
  leans his head on his hand.*)

    Enter SYBIL.

  Old A. (*recognizing her as she approaches*). Miss
  Cooper!
Can it be (*in a low voice*)?

  Sybil. It is. (*Aside.*) Old Acton of Eaglemont.
Go where I will, some ghost of that dread spot
Haunts me in human form.

There's some mistake, sir, I seek the lawyer,
Mr. William Acton.

 Old A. My son—no mistake.

 Sybil. Your son, sir !

 Old A. Yes, my son, and your old friend.
He is here—William.

>   (*Sybil approaches a few steps towards William
>   Acton, he turns round—they recognize.*)

 Sybil (*aside*). William Ashley ! (*To him*) You know
  me, Mr. Acton,
I see you know me.

 Acton. Could I forget you !

 Sybil. Not forget, perhaps : but—but—
Of course you know my person ;—who I was,
But—not who I am.

 Acton. Yes, that I know.

 Sybil. Thank heaven ! Something then is spared
  me !

 Acton. I know the whole sad story, Margaret—
Mistress Clifden. Can *I* do thee service (*with emotion*) ?
Is it for this you seek me !

 Sybil. It is.

 Acton. I'm ready. All that lies within my power
You can command. Most necessary 'tis
That I immediately your husband see.

 Sybil. Cannot that be avoided—I know all.

 Acton. Your husband's danger I'll not hide from you.
Society is sick of deeds of blood,
And will, I fear, exact law's coldest rigor.

 Sybil (*eagerly*). But the provocation of the villain
Whom he slew—what have I said !

 Acton. What you have said, you have in secret said :
Your husband well doth know the lawyer's need,

To do him justice I must see himself :
To meet the worst, his friends must know the worst.
And I will see him—I'm thy friend and his.

  Sybil (*aside*). Eustace cannot refuse me when he's
   there.

'Tis best. I thank thee deeply, William Ashley—
I feel I don't deserve this at thy hands.
Thou art avenged for all the past. (*Weeps.*)

  Acton.   Margaret,
I need no such atonement. To see thee thus
Brings me no feelings but of stubborn pain,
Which cannot in thy misery be tamed.
Oh, such a youth—such pride of promise.

  Sybil. Ay, indeed, such pride!—Such pride, and such
   a fall.

  Acton. But is there not hope still—

  Sybil. For *him?* You will save him?

  Acton. I will try.

  Sybil. I know you will—you must ! But even then
I sometimes think there is no hope on earth.
I am a wreck. If I outlive this storm,
'Twill be as a craft hereafter useless.
These storms have shattered me. I fear my brain
Will, like the hurricane, sweep wildly out,
And leave my head as empty as the space
'Twixt earth and sky, to either not allied—
Or filled with fathomless wild clouds, that give
Terror to earth below, in shutting out
All hopeful specks of heaven above.

    [*Old Acton, who has been a quiet spectator, wipes
      away a tear, and exits silently.*

  Acton. Hope is the sustenance of youth, and you
Are young.

Sybil.　　　I've faith in you.　I always had
Reliance on your truth.
　　Acton.　　　　　　Had you believed so *then*—
　　Sybil. I did believe so.
　　Acton.　　　　　　Could you have thought—
　　Sybil (*trembling*). No more—say no more.
　　Acton (*half musing*). Could it have been, there had
　　　　been now no wreck.
　　Sybil (*with stern frenzy*). Speak not thus.　The past
　　　　is past.
It could not have been otherwise.　There was
A fate to humble me, and I am humbled.
I am here to sue, to beg *your* succor.
'Tis best so.　*You* have nothing to deplore.
Oh, William—William (*seizes him*) ! forget the past—
Or, if you still will cling unto those days,
Remember them to save him, for *my* sake.
Save him—my life, my husband.　Come—come—come—
Each moment from him is a lifetime now.　　　[*Exeunt.*

　　　　　SCENE III.—*Dungeon, as before.*

Enter CLIFDEN, SYBIL, *and* JAILER.　JAILER *exit, and
　　closes the door upon them.　Noise of bolts.*

　　Clif. (*embraces Sybil*). The ordeal's past that I most
　　　　feared to meet.
The trial than the sentence has more dread,
To one who fears death less than scrutiny.
To be the gaze of every sottish boor
Who hiccoughs jeers and damns me for a fool ;
The criticised of cold and upright knaves
Who knit their brows in reverence of laws
They daily break, and say " how bold he looks—

The murderer ;" the fashionable chat
Of fellows whose weak lives are lust, whose dreams
Are drunken echoes of their days, and who
In self-defence must say " he looks a villain ;"
The topic for those philanthropic dogs
Who bark at every thing, and never bite,
Who'd let the vilest progeny of hell
Loose on the earth that they might rail against them ;—
To be this ; hemmed in a dock, the bars of which
Have propp'd up every crime that law and gold,
Thirst, madness, tainted blood, foul head, black heart,
Or tortured nature e'er invented ;—this
Gives a shock to make a pure man quake.
But it is over—the dread trial's past,
And I'm prepared.   The verdict cannot bring
Aught but relief.

    Sybil (*doubtfully*). Does not the defence bring hope ?
With all my actuality of wrong
I never knew how great the villain was,
My own infirmity, or your great soul,
Till Acton set in dreadfulest display
The picture 'fore my eyes.

    Clif.   A brave, bright soul !
Upon whose brow great nature's mark is good.
As nobly balanced as the poles, as wide
Of heart, and fathomless in honesty
As the deep sea, whose currents, ever fresh,
Play with the leaded line that seeks its depth.

    Sybil. And when with such calm emphasis he rose
To the laws venue, and declared that he,
Knowing the vulture passions of the dead,
Would not have held your weapon from the act
That sent a life's debts to be paid above,

I could have worshipped him before all eyes
But that *his* speech did choke all words for mine.
Oh, Clifden, how his words drag down my brain
With thoughts which taunt me with my selfish ends.
Have mercy on me—pardon my hot blood
That fused your genius to my vengeance.
Forgive me, husband, for nor earth nor heaven
Will come between me and the odious sin.

 Clif. (*putting his arm about her*). Sybil, my own—my
  beautiful—my bride—
Look in my face, and see if there's a line
By which you may not trace my heart's proud boast—
That you're my wife! (*Noise of bolts. They watch the
  door.*)

    Enter WILLIAM ACTON.

 Sybil (*rushes towards Acton and falls on her knees*). If
  the full prayers of one like me can reach
The throne, they are *there* pleading for you now.
 Acton. Rise, Margaret (*raising her*)—rise : 'tis not for
  you to kneel
To me.
 Clif. How can I measure my poor thanks
To fill your measureless exertions !
 Acton. Were the deed mine, I know you would have
  stood
In my defence where I have stood in yours,—
That is thanks enough for me. But the court
Waits ; the jury have returned.
 Sybil. So soon! (*Startled.*)
 Clif. I am ready.
 Sybil (*to Acton*). What prospect !—Did they bear
Acquittal on their faces ? Did they seem

As though their hearts throbbed with a good deed?
Or did their eyes see corpses in the air?
Say, say.   Did they breathe freely, or held up,
Lest they might lack enough of breath to float
That grave-stone sentence—"Guilty!"   Ah, I feel
My life is slipping through their hands.
   Clif. We attend the court (*going*).
   Acton. 'Tis better that your wife remain. (*Sybil listens.*)
   Sybil (*screams*). Then all is lost!
      (*Clifden kisses her; she struggles to go with him;*
         he gently disengages her, and hurries out after
         Acton.   Sybil falls on her knees in agony.)
   Sybil (*after a pause, gazing up wildly*). What say
      you—Guilty, or Not Guilty?
Stay, stay—hear me!   Old man, your looks are kind—
You have a daughter; ah! I knew you had,
There is such tender comfort in your eye.
I had a father once: take care, old man,
Your comfort may not wither 'neath the touch
Of the destroyer.   Ha! you shake your head:
But look at me—who thought that I could fall?
Old man, beware!   Your heartlessness makes way
For such as dragg'd me down.   Go, go!
You have a sister, sir; protect the man
Who has protected her!   You smile to think
She needs protection;—Fool! all women do.
You will not speak to me—go to, coward.
And you;—but no, there's earth about your eyes—
They're clay: debauch has settled on your cheek;
Time's very precious, I cannot speak with you.
Nor you, thou low-browed homily on man.
But here, I have a man, and married too?
'Tis well!   He'll feel for me!   What think you now—

Your bosom friend comes glozing round your wife
And seeks to raise such hellish flames in her
As leave you but in ashes—Eh—eh ?
Kill him you would ? Brave husband ! Then say which—
" Guilty," or " Not Guilty ?"   Speak it loud—loud—
That your good presence may inspire these knaves.
Gone—where is my good friend gone ?   All are going !
Stay—look at this youth, my husband : think you
He committed murder—ha ! ha ! He ? No !
He *did ?* I say he did not ! What a world
Of men, fathers, brothers, husbands—all gone.
Where is my Clifden ?   Gone too (*screams*)—they've
      taken him
To death—the gallows ! (*Cheering outside.*) Hear how
      the rabble shout
To see a brave man die.   Oh Clifden !—husband !

Enter CLIFDEN, ACTON, MAUDE, JANETTE, MR. LOWE,
      MRS. HARDY.

   Voices outside. Not guilty !
   Sybil (*rushing to Clifden*). Not guilty (*falls into his
      arms*)—not guilty ! Did I hear aright ?
   Clif. Yes, dearest Sybil—yes.   I am here—free !
   Sybil. Free !   Oh (*a long sigh*), this great joy has
      ta'en the little life
My sorrow left.   Forgive me, William :
Kiss me, dear mother—sisters, fare ye well.
Oh, do not leave me, Eustace ;—Let me feel you near—
Close to my heart, my husband :—Come,—come.
I cannot see you now—there is a film
Hovering o'er my sight.   Eustace, good-by !
Have mercy, heaven !—" Not—Guilty." (*Sinks.*)
            (*Slow music as curtain descends.*)

SYBIL—CAST OF CHARACTERS.

	ST. LOUIS THEATRE. September 6, 1858.	LOUISVILLE, KY.
Eustace Clifden	MR. CHARLES POPE.	MR. KEEBLE.
Rufus Wolfe	" HAMBLIN.	" RILEY.
Old Acton	" GRIFFITHS.	" TOWNSEND.
William Acton	" WRIGHT.	" DICKSON.
Mr. Lowe	" HIND.	" LORTON.
Barnabas	" F. PAIGE.	" WM. SCALLAW
Landlord of the Red Heifer	" KLONE.	
Gentlemen	" PENNOYER.	
Sybil Hardy	MISS AVONIA JONES.	MISS AVONIA JONES.
Mrs. Hardy	MRS. F. S. BUXTON.	MRS. GILBERT.
Maude Clifden	" PENNOYER.	MISS IRENE WALKER.
Janette		" IDA VERNON.

	ST. CHARLES. New Orleans, 1859.	MOBILE, ALA.
Eustace Clifden	MR. CHAS. POPE.	MR. HANLEY.
Rufus Wolfe	" HAMBLIN.	" RALTON.
Old Acton	" GRIFFITHS,	" CURRAN.
William Acton	" WRIGHT.	" ASHMED.
Mr. Lowe		
Barnabas	" F. PAIGE.	" RAYMOND.
Landlord of the Red Heifer	" KRONE.	
Gentlemen		
Sybil Hardy	MISS AVONIA JONES.	MISS AVONIA JONES.
Mrs. Hardy	MRS. F. S. BUXTON.	" BERREL.
Maude Clifden	MISS PENNOYER.	MRS. LINGARD.
Janette	" FANNY DENHAM.	" H. BERNARD.

	OPERA HOUSE. San Francisco.	METROPOLITAN. Sacramento, Cal.
Eustace Clifden	MR. LEWIS BAKER.	MR. LEWIS BAKER.
Rufus Wolfe	" KINGSLAND.	" KINGSLAND.
Old Acton	" MORTIMER.	" MORTIMER.
William Acton	" COAD.	" COAD.
Mr. Lowe	" THOMAN.	" THOMAN.
Barnabas	" DUMPHRIES.	" GLOVER.
Landlord of the Red Heifer	" McCABE.	" MACKLIN.
Gentlemen	" THAYER.	
Sybil Hardy	MISS AVONIA JONES.	MISS AVONIA JONES.
Mrs. Hardy	MRS. JUDAH.	" NELLIE BROWN.
Maude Clifden	MISS COGSWELL.	" COGSWELL.
Janette	" JENNIE MANDEVILLE.	" J. MANDEVILLE.

	WINTER GARDEN. New York.	WALNUT STREET Philadelphia.
Eustace Clifden	MR. BARTON HILL.	MR. LAWRENCE P. BARRETT
Rufus Wolfe	" J. J. PRIOR.	" E. L. TILTON.
Old Acton	" JEFFRIES.	" G. JOHNSON
William Acton	" A. H. DAVENPORT.	" WRIGHT.
Mr. Lowe	" W. DAVIDGE.	" B. YOUNG.
Barnabas	" C. WALCOT, JR.	" BASCOMBE.
Landlord of the Red Heifer.	" STYLES.	" PORTER.
Gentlemen	{ " J. H. EVANS. " CLARKE.	" RAYMOND. " MATTHEWS.
Sybil Hardy	MISS MATILDA HERON.	MRS. EMMA WALLER.
Mrs. Hardy	MRS. WALCOT.	MISS WOOD.
Maude Clifden	MISS ANNIE WILKS.	" JOSEPHINE TYSON.
Janette	" FANNY BROWNE.	" JOHNSON.

HOWARD ATHENÆUM.
Boston.

Eustace Clifden	MR. JAMES DUFF.
Rufus Wolfe	" F. E. AIKEN.
Old Acton	
William Acton	
Mr. Lowe	
Barnabas	
Landlord of the Red Heifer.	
Gentlemen	
Sybil Hardy	MRS. EMMA WALLER.
Mrs. Hardy	
Maude Clifden	MISS M. NEWTON.
Janette	

The casts at many prominent city theatres—such as those at Richmond, Cincinnati, Chicago, Memphis, Nashville, Providence, and other minor places in the United States, and Melbourne, Australia, were unattainable.

COPYRIGHT PRIVILEGE.

Managers or actors desirous of producing this drama will communicate with the author, care of the Publisher, New York.

EVA: A GOBLIN ROMANCE.

IN FIVE PARTS.

ROBERT SHELTON MACKENZIE, D. C. L.

MY DEAR DOCTOR :—

I feel a pardonable pride in offering you this little book. Were its merits but equal to the gratification experienced in dedicating it to you, its reputation would be a foregone conclusion, and only make me more happy that it was in some degree worthy of your acceptance. I pray you, however, to take it, such as it is, as a small token of my appreciation of your indefatigable labors in the cultivation and dissemination of a healthy and hearty Polite Literature, of your high sense of professional independence, and of your generosity to professional juniors—a generosity the more gladly recorded here because I have been a partaker of its fruits.

Among contemporary writers, I am not aware of any more ready to welcome and endorse what your judgment recognizes as deserving; or who, being forced into an opposite course, justifies his disapproval out of resources more complete, or by standards more compatible with common sense and the dignity of letters. These characteristics, so widely valued and respected, fortify the desire of personal regard to inscribe this romance with your name.

A word as to the work itself. While illustrating the plot— if I may call it such—by the resources Fancy and Imagination conjure up as lying within the supernatural and fairy realms, and by the reflection of the scenery, occasion, and moods of the actors upon each other, I have attempted—like an old-fashioned story-teller—more than once to point a moral; and in the con-

1*

cluding part, to lead the mind to dwell on the still higher, more enduring, and more consoling teaching of Christianity, that, amid the vicissitudes which rack man—not the least crushing of which is a transition from the egotistic rapture of a passionate young love to the humiliating consciousness of moody despair—his only comfort and lasting reward is to be found in the self-sacrifice, the resignation—in a word—the humble, but heroic virtues symbolized by THE CROSS.

Accept, my dear Doctor, this dedication, with the affectionate esteem of

Your Friend,   .

JOHN SAVAGE.

FORDHAM, *September* 25, 1865.

E V A.

PART FIRST.

I.

The evening Sun was setting fair
  Beneath a sky of blue,
And Nature's charms on earth, in air,
  Were fading into dew:

II.

The sun's broad beams athwart did lie
  The crimson-mantled West,
As a golden Cross of Chivalry
  Charged on a purple vest:

III.

The evening star, with tender freight
  Of charitable mirth,
Did seem to cheer and gratulate
  The day-tired sons of earth.

IV

A gentle breath the shrubs among—
  A gentle sigh of air.
As though a gentle maiden's song
  Was lilting here and there;

V.

The busy bushes keeping time,
  The tendrils join each note,
And all is soft as silv'ry rhyme
  From out a silv'ry throat:

VI.

The grass assumes a whimpering thrill
  As through it wings the wind,
So gently though, it scarcely speeds
To coax a chorus from yon weeds,
  Ere all is still behind:

VII.

The dry stems wheeze a tiny pipe
   To show they wakeful lie,
As urchins mumble unknown type
   When pedagogue struts by :

VIII.

The wild rose blushes on the eve
   Of going to its rest,
And bends its crimson cheek to grieve
   On mother Earth's calm breast.

IX.

The dew steals o'er primroses pale
   Which deck yon shady place;
And clustering in a shy delight,
Help to shake the tears of night
   From off each others' face :

X.

And hawthorn blossoms titter low,
   For fear their joyaunce reach
The matron-like and crabbed boughs,
While am'rous Air essays its vows
   And steals a kiss from each :

XI.

The mountain Ash, gay lithe and young.
 With knowledge of its grace,
Unheedful hears the gallant's song,
Nor cares be won by secret tongue,
 It bends to bolder face.

XII.

The evening calm as the smile of Him,
 Who said, " Thy Will be done,"
And the pious air seemed hushed in prayer
 Like a seraphic nun.

XIII.

The scene was wild, yet Fancy made
 Its features full of balm
As though it joined the lengthening shade
 To make the day's death calm.

XIV.

In truth it was a placid scene
 Where awe did wonder woo:
Yea, such as men full seldom ken
 The coming twilight through.

XV.

It is a brocken valley wild,
  The Dodder streaming down
Its centre, and the mountain heath
Envelops with a purple wreath
  Kippure's age-mottled crown.

XVI.

O valley! consecrate to song,
  In poet-warrior's soul,
Where memories of Ossian throng—
  Delightful Glan-nis-mole![1]

XVII.

O valley! famed in Ancient days
  Not more by Ossian's voice,
Than thrushes', whose bewildering maze
Of melody made all thy braes
  And hundred dells rejoice.

XVIII.

Romantic, rugged, sombre, grand,
  The hills jut out and fall
Into the devious vale, as though
To stay the Dodder's reckless flow ;
  Which, foams, and frets, through all.

XIX.

They drive the stream from shore to shore;
　　It shakes with rage, then sweeps
Around the base, with lengthening pace,
With sullen surge, breaks through the gorge,
　　And frothing, onward leaps.

XX.

By Alyagower, clear as glass
　　The pools glide smoothly free,
Till further down, a group of rocks,
Like bathing dwarfs, jumps up and mocks
　　Their placid ecstasy.

XXI.

Then like branch-broken rays from sun—
　　Or sparks from the blacksmith's blow—
Or, shattered gems, they flash and run
　　To frothen the angry flow.

XXII.

And now they chant a boisterous song,
　　United, now they hymn,
And anon they murmuring lilt along
　　In the shade of yon brocken, dim.

XXIII.

The brave ship many leagues must tack
    As air and ocean wills:
So strove the river, making track
    Athrough this sea of hills.

XXIV.

An ivy-quilted scanty ruin
    Lies hugged i' the valley wild;
And tombs there tell, of all save hell
    To martyr, man, and child.

XXV.

In the shade of the lonely pile,
    Like life within a dream,
In the shade of the holy aisle
    A listening to the stream—

XXVI.

A listening to the Dodder's woes
    A-neath the ivy green,
A damsel and youth, the like in sooth
    I'm sure you ne'er have seen.

XXVII.

Ye sprites, it was a dreamy scene .
　　And a witching wild one, too,
Such as we but seldom see,
　　The elfin twilight through.

XXVIII.

The youthful maid an angel's face—
　　And angel's form, I ween,
A mingling grace lit up her face
　　Of blooming ripe sixteen.

XXIX.

Tresses like an autumn night
　　Hang o'er her forehead's day,
Darkly rich—a pearly light
　　Outlines each curling spray

XXX.

Eyes of such unearthly light,
　　Though dark as ever wrought;
By Heaven! they twist me as a sprite,
　　Though I but see in thought.

XXXI.

Much more they twisted yon poor soul,
　The brave youth by her side,
Whose pupils rise to the maid's dark eyes
And in the wild glance dies, and dies
　To live in hopeful pride.

XXXII.

He sighs, that wily nature should
　Play freaks to show her might,
And make in witching maidenhood
　The darkest eyes most bright.

XXXIII.

Her forehead, as white marble, pale,
　The veins an azure river,
Where tints of Ireland's skies prevail
　In softness, softening ever.

XXXIV.

Her cheeks, the dainty tenderness
　As when at morning's dawn,
The sun-beam is shed, through a rose-leaf, red,
　On a neighboring ccanavaun.[2]

XXXV.

Her lips! a healthy pure repast—
  A sylph's or mortal's, which?
The upper like the bright spring cast,
  The under autumn rich:

XXXVI.

And both control a fragrant breath
  Like breeze o'er summer flowers,
When jocund morn enliveneth
  Earth's re-awakened powers.

XXXVII.

Her voice was like a happy thought
  Whose speaking smile did sun you,
And ere you heard the opening word
  The movement had undone you.

XXXVIII.

A raiment white with girdle green
  Her dainty waist about,
For as her heart was pure within,
  Her garb was pure without.

XXXIX.

So take the fair for all in all :
   Such a pure though tempting smile,
Ne'er shone from maid
As on him who strayed
   Through that old monastic aisle.

XL.

Comely shaped the youth, and slender ;
   With four summers o'er her own :
    And ever since they gambolled
    On the hill-paths over-brambled,
In sunny childhood's days, the tender
   Passion, with their growth had grown.

XLI.

Never slept it : for their sleeping
   Ne'er was by its dreams forsaken—
    Sleep, our Nature's El Dorado,
    Only held it by a shadow—
While they gathered golden dream-tales
   To be told when they'd awaken.

XLII.

Thus their nights were but as segments
    Of the circle of their days;
And their young hearts, sunny centres,
    Rich with Love's converging rays.

XLIII.

Young Kevin Dhu, so was he hight,
    For ay, was youth as good
As e'er bent bow on Saxon foe,
Or boasted the commingling flow
    Of Celto-Norman blood.

XLIV.

His voice is full and freshly clear
    As the breeze on Comm'ragh's crown;
His hand can harp to a maiden's ear
    Or strike a foeman down.

XLV.

The brown locks cluster on his brow,
    Like grapes on the brow of Pan,
And you see a man in the youth though now
    The youth is scarcely man.

XLVI.

Lonely looks the ancient pile;
　But love is lonely never,
When loving eyes exchange the while
　The arrows from Love's quiver.

XLVII.

Solemn the weird and lonely scene,
　Solemn the tombs arraigned—
It looks as Life had all buried been,
　And they alone remained.

XLVIII.

In truth, it was a holy scene,
　And a lonely wild one too,
Such as men full seldom ken
　The dusky twilight through.

XLIX.

A harp, Love's vibrant symbol, rude
　In shape, but sweet in tone,
Lay o'er a tomb, as though its mood
　Was dirging the dead alone.

L.

She sate her down upon a tomb,
    A cross rose high before,
With mossy shapes from Time's gray womb,
    Emboss'd and stainèd o'er.

LI.

"What hopes!" he cried, "what love, what truth,
    These ancient crosses speak!
What chastening thoughts for strength and
      youth,
    What sinews for the weak!

LII.

"With Vandal Time, their Sculptures rude
    But sacred combat well;
Like trusty friends, they have outstood
    The wealth that from us fell.

LIII.

"'Twould seem the centuried bones beneat
    With strength of faith had grown
To mark the true soul's hope in death,
    And rose in sculptured stone.

LIV.

" Ye granite graybeards of the past
　　Who watch our kindred o'er,
With us may e'er thy teachings last,
　　That we the Cross adore.

LV.

" These crosses, like great note-marks, stand
　　O'er all the Celtic sod,
Grown gray in agony of love
　　Referring us to God !"³

LVI.

And then, as dropping in the tide
　　Of thought his fervor sprung,
The youth in Celtic anguish sighed
　　Its mysty waves among.

LVII.

'Twas but a moment, though it seemed,
　　In retrospection, years,
And waking from the life he dreamed—
　　Ancestral blood and tears—

LVIII.

He leaned against the carven cross,
   That rood of holy stone,
In love's weird tremors both at loss,
   To claim each heart their own.

LIX.

He brushed his brow, he snatched his harp,
   A prelude wildly rang;
Then melting to a plaintive width
   Of soul, he to her sang:

(I.)

A love-lorn minstrel once there dwelt,
   In a valley fair to view,
Whose young rapt soul and senses knelt,
   A heavenly maid to woo.
His love was fierce as Saint Kevin's hate,[4]
   Pure as yon spring of Saint Ann,—
He loved with the fervor soul doth create,
   As a minstrel only can.

(II.)

He roamed like spirit called from earth,
   Chimed from its grave·of rest,

Penance to eke for some worldlie mirth,
  Or for some act unblest:
For his love was fierce as Saint Kevin's hate,
  Killing as e'en the Saint's ban:
Oft voiceless, his was an ideal state
  Of loving, as minstrel can.

(III.)

He tracked her steps, o'er vale and hill,
  True as the shadow she made;
He blessed the sod whereon she trod,
  And the breeze that round her played.
For never to him had the sense of sound
  So lovingly tender grown,
As when the air, caressing the fair,
  Partook of her dulcet tone.

(IV.)

The Holy Well at which she drank
  To him more holy grew
Each tree that gave her shade, each bank
  She rested on, he knew!
For he gazed on his love as Martyr would
  On the hope that raised his soul,
And his eyes to her rolled as the halo should
  Round the head of the Virgin roll.

(v.)

Oh, this maid was his sole divinity!
   A model for aye far above
Aught his brain, in its minstrel affinity
   To heaven, could weave for his love!
And he loved her as Kate loved Saint Kevin,
   And he traced her as dial the sun;
For at morning, at noon, or at even,
   By either you'd find t'other one.

(vi.)

And though they had gambolled in youthhood,
   From childhood to each other clung,
Yet neither had strength in their truthhood,
   Nor perfectly freedom of tongue:
For love, when it grows up from childhood,
   Ne'er thinks to seek deeper the clue,
But looks on each face as the wildwood,
   Where unconscious their heart-flowers grew.

(vii.)

And though he had laughed forth his fancies,
   And though she reëchoed his tale,
Yet for *one* word each heart inward glances—
   That one word of blessing or bale.

LX.

" Ah, sad is the time!" spake Eva,
 " When hearts are unconsciously tost;
'Twere better that one should have spoken
 Than voiceless that both should be lost.

LXI.

" Ah," sighed she, " I pain for the maiden!"
 " And I," quoth he, " wail for the youth!"
" And did neither make them an Aiden,
 By shriving the other from ruth?

LXII.

" And did neither think of presuming
 On friendship that from their birth grew?"
" Ah, no!" said the young bard resuming
 His harp, and its love-burdened clue:

" Though the youth but in her saw his heaven,
 Still spake not, or heard not *the word*;
For," he faltered, " the youth's name was KEVIN,
 And—EVA, the maid he adored!"

3

LXIII.

With modest, not unconscious air,
    Dear Eva heard him close : —
And looked, but spoke not, worlds of prayer,
    That only true love knows.

LXIV.

She felt—she knew, she had *his* heart,
    And that it spake through her,
And waited her responsive part
    From *him*,—nor dared to stir,—

LXV.

Nor dared to stir, lest she displace
    The accents she well knew
Her heart must make; but woke apace
    To her own maiden view.

LXVI.

" Ah, Kevin! in my maiden soul
    Is the heart that I bereft
Thee of—that I, unconscious, stole,—
    Yet, willing for the theft:

LXVII.

"Ay, willing for the theft! O youth,
　　O Kevin dear! 'tis frail
That Eva's tongue should tell; but truth
　　And love's a sad tell-tale."

LXVIII.

" Angel of Eva! let me hear
　　Those kindling thoughts again;
That Hope's clear light may shame the bier
　　Where chilling Doubt lies slain!"

LXIX.

"My Kevin dear, fain would I tell,—
　　My tongue but shames its place,
My lips but mock the inward spell
　　That needs would outward trace.

LXX.

"My heart is throbbing like a sea,
　　And could sea span the skies above,
I feel its vast immensity
　　Could not cradle half my love."

LXXI.

Entrancèd in her speech, he gazed
  As though a statue still—
Or like a breathless sculptor, dazed
  At his creative skill.

LXXII.

But suddenly he started,—bright,
  His thankful gestures spoke,
As vocal as a host of light,
  In cave dawn never woke.

LXXIII.

His harp fell on the tufted moss,
  His tongue seemed in his fingers,[5]
That motion all his words,—at loss
  While speech on his dumb mouth lingers

LXXIV.

He wrapt her to his burning breast,
  That love should fear no cheating;
He prest her, that each pledging test
  Should feel each other beating.

LXXV.

Exchangèd troths of love were given,
   And Echo sealed each tone,
Before the Cross, and the holy heaven,
   In the ivied ruin lone.

3*

PART SECOND.

I.

As thus the pair entrancèd were,
　Each with the other's love;
Unseen, unheard, about them there
　A horrid pageant wove.

II.

Old name-lost tombs 'gan start to life—
　The dead 'gan hobbling out,
Martyrs and monks, and man and wife,
　To witness what they're about.

III.

As lumberingly moved the mounds
　That did the ground encumber,
The headstones cracked their lichen skins,
　And yawn'd, like sots in slumber.

IV.

Old battered memories on the walls,
   Took shape and left their places;
Crushed effigies in crumbling stalls,
   Resumed their forms and faces.

V.

And skeletons helped with rattling noise
   To empty each other's graves,
To witness the troth and hear the voice
   Of love that daintily raves.

VI.

The oldest trees did shake and quake
   Up to their farthest shoots,
     As each skeleton pulls
     Might and main for the skulls,
Meshed in the tangled roots.

VII.

You'd think it was a lashing hail
   Upon the branching eaves;
Or wild despoiling autumn gale
   A throttling all the leaves.

VIII.

And while the groups are gathering round
  From out their dim abodes,
The woes and state of some create
  Grim ghastly episodes.

IX.

A horrid shape from the path to hell
  Escaped to quench his thirst,
For his inside scorch'd as flames do dwell
  In house pent ere they burst.

X.

He came to drink of the mystic Well
  Blessed by the good Saint Ann,
Whose waters boast the purest spell
  From Tallaght to Lough Dan.[6]

XI.

And deftly to the holy pool
  This ghastly shape forsooth
Did speed, with shrinèd wave to cool
  His hellish scorching drouth.

XII.

He snatched the bowl from the holy stone,
 And dived it in the Well;
  But yet while there flew
  His parched frame through
 A bliss from the hoped-for spell,
  A hurrying sprite
  Dashed the cup from his sight,
And he felt o'er again pangs of hell.

XIII.

Oh could he but drink of the shriving wave,
 'Twould give him the freedom of soul
To think of a heav'n; his body 'twould save
From the torturing pangs of a hell-bound grave:
 He snatches again at the bowl.

XIV.

Is it Saint Ann? or a guarding band?
 Or hath he a soul conscience-barred?
Again the cup from his flaming hand
 Is dashed by some unseen guard—

XV.

And a voice, like the rending of great forest oaks,
  Begat on his ear, with a yell,
The sentence of Fate—"Hence slave to your
    state
  And your purgatorial cell."

XVI.

He shrunk aback, as his head had been
  Clove with Saint Peter's key,
And he durst not look, for bell and book
  Had told him where he would be.

XVII.

And a group kept watching a tomb in the aisle,
And they grinned a wrathful, vengeful smile,
    In wait for its inmate's skull;
        For he was a lord,
        Whose only word
        Was of hate to the poor,
        And death to the boor
        Who made not his door
And halls with venison full;

XVIII.

And oft had this baron been known to brag,
　　The number of vassals he clove with his mace ;
And he took less delight racing after the stag,
　　Than he did in staying the human race.

XIX.

And one yelled forth a merry stave,
　　A hundred choruss'd the verse ;
　　　And from under a cowl,
　　　A relentless jowl
　　Mumbled a hopeful curse.

XX.

And one whose flesh was half decayed
　　Poured forth a troublous groan,
Which shook the slime from his wormy side,
　　And bared it to the bone.

XXI.

Some had on cerements gray, which flapped
　　As loose sails on the spars of a ship ;
And some, half-rotted on what they wrapped,
　　Were as cobwebs caught on a chip.

XXII.

One looked at her tomb as at her glass,
　Ne'er doubting herself 'twould bear,
　　But she yelled her joy
　　At the fond foul lie
Her husband had sculptured there.

XXIII.

And calling a troupe of like wild wives,
　She bade them see themselves—
All scampered away as they did in their lives—
　A pack of mad vain elves.

XXIV.

And they laughed, did this brood of wanton
　　wives,
　At their sculptured acts, and cried—
"Ho! ho! for those who have led good lives,
　They'll have no surprise when they've died."

XXV.

And as the "Yes" from Eva's mouth
　Proclaimed young Kevin's bride,
All swirled as though the grapes of the South
　Were gurgling their skulls inside.

4

XXVI.

And a jolly mob around the pair
    Prankt madly in a reel,
And chattered, and bowed, and flattered aloud,
    The lovers with devilish zeal.

XXVII.

But lovers' eyes, though ope are blind,
    And lovers' ears are deaf;
'Tis but in loving lovers find
    Love's grief or love's relief.

XXVIII.

Young Kevin clasped the maid again,
    The embrace was soft and sweet;
The bubbling love of the wooers twain,
    At parting was as they'd meet.

XXIX.

And as love's tender stupor sheds
    Its filmy mask, they thought
The air was dotted with strange heads,
    And with strange noises fraught.

XXX.

Their skinny digits clasping fast,
  The mouldy dancers spin
Swiftly past—their skulls are cast
  Into one circling grin.

XXXI.

The fluttering Eva nestled close
  Unto her Kevin's breast,—
They soothed the sudden fears that rose,
  By being both caressed.

XXXII.

"The noise"—it was the weary breeze,
  Or Dodder's plaining tones:
"The faces"—moonshine through the trees
  Upon the quaint old stones.

XXXIII.

And wilder, swifter speed the wraiths,
  As on a whirlpool leaves,
Until they fade, and the speering maid
  Feels she herself deceives.

XXXIV.

The moon breaks from her camp of clouds,
  And roams the clear expanse;
The ghosts glide into their slimy shrouds,
  Tired with the trysting dance.

PART THIRD.

I.

The moon was taking her highest roll,
   And the light from her regnant head,
Enwrapped the stars, like a mighty scroll,
   With eternity's language spread.

II.

The crystal blue of the ambient sky,
   The crystal light of the moon,
The crystal note of the black-bird nigh,
   Makes echo a crystal tune.

III.

The stars like strings of a heavenly lyre,
   Swept by the hands of Night,
Fill with joy the cathedral choir;
   And echo is turned to light.

4*

IV.

And down the moonlight flutes the air,
  Each beam a choral column;
And earth's calm but responsive prayer
  Blends in the midnight solemn.

V.

And heavenly smiles and earthly thanks
  In their descent and upward flight,
Pass in joyed and bowèd ranks
  Through night's corridors of light.

VI.

The wakeful crags, Kippure's broad brow
  Stand out in bright relief,
Attendant on the moon; and throw
  The glens in shadowed grief.

VII.

Scarce a stir was up in the air,
  Scarce a stir on the earth,
Save lyrical rills from the elfin hills
  Gamb'lling in wildsome mirth.

VIII.

They staved and raved adown the stones,
    A stop-note every pebble,
To quiver the chant into tinkling tones
    Of a dulcet treble.

IX.

At the time of fair Eva's vows
    To Kevin's love-lit power,
The elfin queen her courtiers did rouse
    To meet over Alyagower.

X.

Bustling, yet noiseless, came along
    The elves from midnight sprees,
Lowly but sweet as ever was song
    They lilted their gathering glees:
So genial the flow, so num'rous the throng,
    It was as a perfumed breeze—
Or, like a forethought of Zephyr's song,
    Balmy, without the breeze.

XI.

As diamond thoughts in quaint bard's brain.
    This aeriel world 'gan float;
And linked, as the gems of a fountain rain
    By the mist. with a dewy note.

XII.

A haze of sound enwrapped the elves
  As the mist o'er a wayward stream ;
They must have thought, the imps themselves,
  They were in an elfin dream.

XIII.

And hither they come, so various dight—
  So brilliant their guises were,
It was as a sudden May that night,
  And they the flow'rs o' the air.

XIV.

Spirit of Heath and Daisy-dew,
  And tiny Blue-bell first,
Bounding came, with the elfin crew,
  That followed in a burst.

XV.

Honey-suckle and Primrose-tip,
  Arm in arm, I wist—
And Evening-sigh and Tulip-lip,
  And the Fog-sprite, Dodder-mist :

XVI.

Jessamine-breath and Woodbine-brow,
  Blessing each other's way,
And Honey-tongue and Folks-glove, now,
  And many a valley fay:

XVII.

The scarlet Dragon's-head came up,
  And Morning-glory too,
Bearing a monstrous purple cup
  Gleaming with nectrous dew:

XVIII.

And Apple-bloom so lustrous white,
  Like little bride of old;
And Dandelion, like ancient king,
  With collar of yellow gold:

XIX.

And from the Dodder's coolest vale
  The Brook-elf, braw and stout,
In armor made of a silver scale
  Dropped from a river trout:

XX.

The imp of glens, wild Thatchet-thorn,
　　Reckless, rollicking sprite,
Came puffing, like a November morn
　　Hunted by autumn night:

XXI.

The Moon-elf with a bright'ning eye,
　　And never a wink, came in;
He trimm'd the starry lamps on high,
　　And shaded the ways of sin.

XXII.

And Poppy-stem with night-cap red,
　　A drowsy pace did take;
But Moon-elf kicked and Thatchet pricked
　　The imp to keep him awake.

XXIII.

And hosts of elfin chiefs appeared
　　Of marvellous renown,
And fairy seannachies[8] with beards
　　Of silver thistle-down.

XXIV.

Oh, myriads came, of goblin fame,
From glen-embower'd ways,
Where cascades keep the hills from sleep,
In witching Wicklow's praise;
From Dodder's nooks, and brawling brooks,
And Liffey's fairy braes.

XXV.

They came to a tower, 'tween heav'n and earth,
Built in the dewy air;
The dreamliest space that fanciful mirth
Could deem for a court so rare.

XXVI.

They carried a cloud away up to the moon
And trailed it across the light,
So the beam from below, and the beam from aboon,
Made a floor and a ceiling bright.

XXVII.

And they sprent the floor with gathered dews
Which shone like a pavement of gems,
And arch'd columns made
Of the clear cascade,
Caught ere it broke in diadems.

XXVIII.

From quarried mines of perfume, the walls—
　　The casement of spider's web, quaint,
　　　And the toiling stars
　　　Snatch a peep through the bars,
　　And pale at their own restraint.

XXIX.

And o'er the throne of Cleena the queen,
　　In the nave of this fairy pile,
　　　A tulip leaf rained
　　　Its hues, like the stained
　　Glass saints in cathedral aisle.

XXX.

Thus met, the queen with an airy tongue,
　　Like a sweet voice heard in a dream,
Half cadenced her will, half liltingly sung—
　　Yet singing it only did seem.

XXXI.

　　Oh, her's was the sweetest,
　　Richest, completest,
　　Most musical, magic, and dearest,
　　Mystic and lowly,
　　Swelling but slowly,
The warmest of voices, and clearest!

XXXII.

" Sisters and brothers—subjects all,
　　From Tallaght to Kippure,
　From the dusky valleys,
　Where the sunset rallies,
　All our gallant armies to my evening call—
　From the heathy hill-side,
　From the dreamy rill-side,
　From the spray entrancing,
　In the star-light glancing,
　O'er the rocky barriers in the Dodder's way,—
　Ye, my loved and loving,
　Ye, the spry and roving,
　Ye, that know a living dead to things of clay,
　Ye, from Tallaght's meadows.
　　To the bleak Kippure,
　Ye, I want—my shadows!
　　A maiden to secure.

XXXIII.

" Cluricauns from haunted Brake,
　　Fays of Alyagower,
　I've a maid from earth to take
　　Worthy fairy power.

5

XXXIV.

" Wild elves from the witch'd Cornaun,
　　Whose broad brow the thunder mocks,
　And all ye that wraithe Glancree,
　　Or guard the lonely haunted Loughs,—⁹

XXXV.

" Where the eagle mountain stands
　　O'er the dismal wave below;
　Like man's suicidal thought
　　Brooding flight from earthly wo:

XXXVI.

" There is a maid of mildest mien,
　　But radiant in its mildness!
　Loving and loved in the bounds atween,
　　Where we hold our wildness."

XXXVII.

" I saw—I spied (and laughed in pride),
　　As I skipt o'er yon ruin,"
　Said Thatchet-thorn, holding his side,
　　" Twain Gaffers there a wooin'."

XXXVIII.

"Ha! ha! Oh Berry," Thatchet scritched,
  "An elf with hum-drum twisting
The other dainty hoyden witched,
  And she said, 'No resisting!'

XXXIX.

"I feth it was a mouthful speck,
  I wiss to see them"—
           "Hold sir,
Chain thy tongue or I'll instant wreck
  Thy chine, for being bold, sir."

XL.

Thatchet sneak'd off in the crowd
  Under the wing of a fly,
And he tickled the fly's kind shroud,
  For tears came in laughter's eye.

XLI.

"As I gamboll'd and caught the dew,"
  Quo' the Queen,—"to deck our halls,
The prancing gnats my chariot drew
  Above yon ivied walls.

XLII.

" Oh, Lily-tint ! Oh, Honey-tongue !
Such a face and form—so airy,
As were those ruins old among !
She should have been a fairy.

XLIII.

" And by her side was a hend youth, who
Was pleading love distressing,
And with harmonious plaining, too,
He charmed the maid's caressing.

XLIV.

" She is too fair for mortal man,
Too bright for earthly life,
More formed for elfin joyaunce than
Queen of a heart-ache strife."

XLV.

(" An' ay, besides," cried Thatchet-thorn,
" 'Twill wrath the youth most drearily,
For which I'd spree ten moons to see—
An' that I would most cheerily !")

XLVI.

" We must save her! we must have her,
　　Ere the dews of evening fall,
On to-morrow, and I'll borrow
　　All your freaks to aid my call."
　　　　" Ho! ho!" yell'd, merrily, Thatchet.

XLVII.

" We must save her! we must have her,
　　Ere the lovers meet again,
And we'll bring her, and we'll sing her
　　Fairy songs of soothing strain."
　　　　" I fecks we will!" quo' Thatchet.

XLVIII.

" And we'll charm her, but not harm her,
　　To forget all ties of earth;
For we'll spell-bind, ay, and well bind
　　All our arts to cause her mirth."
　　　　" An' I'm your man!" quo' Thatchet.

XLIX.

" We, you Thatchet-thorn commission—
　　Thatchet list, you wayward wight—
To bethink and twist our wish on
　　Witching this young maiden bright.
5*

L.

" Good lack, ah me! ho, ho !—What now ?"'
   Laughed Thatchet—"*That's* your measure !"
And he smoothed a wrinkle on old Time's brow
   With a loud smack of pleasure.

LI.

The wily, revelling devil, Thorn,
   Swung wild in a cobweb's loop;
A rakish imp as ever was born,
   On the spider he sat with a " Whoop !"

LII.

" All the spreethogue-elves ye ken,
   From Lough Bray to Kill-tipper,
Shall follow Thatchet, through fen and glen,
   To aid the imp to clip her."

LIII.

Thatchet in glee, was tumbling round,
   The cap of a queen-bee's knee;
So joyous was he to be crown'd,
Leading a prank in fairy ground,
   And scritched right gleefully !

LIV.

" Hip, do dun !
    'Tis said—she's won !
I'll smother my feet in the thistle-down,
    Or skate on the snail's bright track,
Or, I'll hide in the pond'rous skin-cloak, brown,
    Flayed from the wood-mouse' back !
Or, I'll straddle on spider's crup, as he weaves
    In the nave of yon ruin his thread—
Or, I'll lie in amidst of two wild mint leaves,
    And roll to a noon-eyed bed.
        I'll watch her—I'll catch her—
            I will ! I will !
        Through alley or valley,
            In bower or hill !
I see her ! I feel her ! I have her ! ha, ha !"
    And he sprang at his joyous note,
    And he laughed, till all doubt
    Such a loud elfin's shout
    Leaped from an elfin throat.

LV.

" Ha ! ha !"—laughed he, as he woke the light
    Of a star that slept on the pavement,
    And he tumbled him round
    To a jocular sound,
Regardless of court behavement.

LVI.

"Hey, in the ruin,
Lovers will be wooing,
Little guessing,
In caressing,
What the elves are doing.

"Hey, in the even,
Lovers will be grieving,
Little knowing
What is growing
For their hearts' deceiving.

"By the set of sun
To-morrow, she's won!

"For o'er the bog,
Or through the fog,
Under the hill,
Over the rill,
In the moonlight,
Or the noonlight,
Bat's wing riding,
Owl's beak chiding,
On Pooka prancing,
Or star-light dancing,

Whatever ye wot
On earth, or be not,
Eft-soon that it *is*,
For Thatchet, I wis,
Is the sprite that is here
To eke whatever ye ken!
For aught be it murky, or yea be it clear—
I'm slave to the Queen o' the glen!
Be it done in a moon's or sun's career,
I'm slave to the Queen o' the glen!"

LVII.

"Hail to our Cleena, Queen o' the glen,"
Shouted the elves and fairy land then,
Up took the echo, and out-sped again—
"Hail to our Cleena, Queen o' the glen."

PART FOURTH.

I.

The night is gone, the morning past,
  And that noon dead forever ;
And evening comes, like a shadow cast,
  Time's brighter tints to sever.

II.

An evening like the yester **one**,
  A calm and balmy eve,
Like nun, afraid that sighing tone
  Would make her bosom heave.

III.

All was still as a sleeping fair,
  Placid with heav'nly dreaming,
Whose visions of bliss to her fancy were
  Double their actual seeming.

IV.

The gentle Eva forth had sped,
　　To meet her idoll'd lover;
The daisy bent not beneath her tread,
　　As Innocence did above her.

V.

Two genial faces-under-a-hood,
　　Drinking the welcome dew,
Seemed, in a joy of brotherhood,
　　Toasting her beauty too.

VI.

The Cowslip and the Buttercup,
　　They bowed a silent bliss,
And Forget-me-not, in the lonely spot,
　　Stole from the sod a kiss.

VII.

Fond memory's emblatic elf,
　　He noted the passing one,
And kissed, in lieu the charmer's self,
　　The ground she trod upon.

VIII.

And thus the plants, in each other's joy,
  Show how they felt for hers,
And kissed once more, as she tript o'er,
  With the zeal of worshippers!

IX.

The meadow-sweet waved like a bridal plume;
  And the streamlet by the path
    Kept on a wild pace,
    To be sunn'd by her face,
Such radiance its beauty hath.

X.

Now was her heart a brimful cup,
  With Love's delicious presence,
And thoughts of Kevin bubbled up
  To the top of the sparkling essence.

XI.

Her bearing bright, her footstep light
  As a May-wafted feather;
She seemed a humanized delight,
  As skipt she o'er the heather.

XII.

And oh, why should she not present
　　Incarnate love and rapture?
Loving and loved—with two joys sprent,
　　Yielding, and making a capture!

XIII.

'Tis only thus that true Love's years
　　Roll free of pain and sin—
The sin of doubt: who happy wears
　　Love's crown, must yield to win.

XIV.

And oh! Heaven help the loving heart
　　That meets no love in turn,
And send its light, to save from blight
　　That passion-bursting urn.

XV.

The heart that links unto a heart,
　　Unknowing if it beats,
May never find, its once clear mind,
　　And peace it never meets—
Earth has no future for its kind;
　　No past, but killing sweets.

XVI.

But Eva, blessing in her love,
　　Was bless'd in her adorer;
The present seem'd but as Peter's gate
　　To the heavenly fate before her.

XVII.

As moved she down the hilly side,
　　Like blossom weather-wafted,
Crowning the air with double pride
　　Of fragrance then engrafted—

XVIII.

A charming strain falls on her ear,
　　A thrilling measure 'tis,
And tender, too.　She stay'd to hear—
　　" Ah! yes, 'tis surely his!

XIX.

" Ah, yes—it must be Kevin's harp!
　　It is that love-lorn strain
He often plays."　She eager stays
　　To catch the loved refrain.

XX.

And yet she stays: adown her head
  Low bent, as joyed she grew,
And hands upraised, as though they said—
  "Hush, birds, and listen too!"

XXI.

The strain swept on—sweet harmony—
  The maiden soul held still,
As though each magic symphony
  Could chain or free at will.

XXII.

"Now shall I give my love surprise!"
  And round she sprang in glee;
But nothing there stood proof her eyes,
  And wonder-struck was she.

XXIII.

Wonder struck was the maiden young,
  At her deceit of ee;
But a voice yet sung, and a harp still rung,
  And still the strain hears she.

XXIV.

Yea, still its ripples lave her ears,
  More dulcet than before,
And every wave of sound she hears
  Is met by an eager shore.

XXV.

Now plaintive rose the witching lay,
  And now a subdued splendor
Trids the dulcet anguish through,
  So passionately tender :

XXVI.

And now a voice of sadness pours
  Its soul upon the air;
While the maiden stays as one delays
  On last words of a prayer.

(.I.)

Where is my darling—
  Oh, where is her shadow?
  Is she in the meadow,
Singing with the starling?

6*

Is she by the river?—
  Is she mid the trees?—
Ah! my heart is ever
  Searching her and ease.

(II.)

I've heard the starling,
  I've been in the meadow,
  But saw not the shadow
Of Eva my darling.
  She's not by the water—
    She's not in the wood—
  Thro' the trees I've sought her,
    And down by the flood.

(III.)

I told the starling
  To sing out my maiden;
  Robin, too, is laden,
With news for my darling;
  And the little sparrow
    That chirps in the thatch,
  And swallow, fleet as arrow,
    Go my love to catch.

(IV.)

I told the starling,
　　Sparrow, and the swallow,
　　Ere they went to follow,
Where *I'd* meet my darling:
Not in fields of clover,
　　Neither in the bower,
Nor by rushing rover,
　　But *here*, at this hour.

XXVII.

" Now shall I give my love surprise !"
　　And round she tript in glee;
But nothing there stood proof her eyes,
　　And wonder struck was she.

XXVIII.

But still the air with song is fraught,
　　Making sweet the gloaming;
'Tis plain the singer's anxious thought
　　But echoes to his roaming.

XXIX.

"Not in fields of clover,
　　Neither in the bower,
Nor by rushing rover,
　　But here, at this hour."

XXX.

Now Eva deftly stole along—
   Softly crept the maiden—
Aside the brake, the shrubs among,
   Her breath love-ful laden.

XXXI.

Scarcely breathing crept she, listening—
   Catching whence the sounds arose;
Her love-laughing eyes were glistening,
   At the sight they will disclose.

XXXII.

Her thoughts were laughing amongst them-
   selves—
   To steal so—such a treat!
Little thought she, the airy elves
   Were laughing at Love's defeat.

XXXIII.

Little she dreamt that an elfin harp,
   Tuned to a mortal ear,
     Was pilf'ring the store,
     At the sill of Love's door,
And making the door a bier.

XXXIV.

"Not in fields of clover,
Neither in the bower,
Nor by rushing rover,
But here, at this hour."

XXXV.

More sorrowful the voice became,
  In grief at her not coming;
Now near it wails, in a tone of blame,
  Now at a distance humming.

XXXVI.

Behind her once it moaned in pain,
  And then it crooned before her;
By her side, anon, as though the strain
  Would weave a madness o'er her.

XXXVII.

On she sprang, with Hope's wild strength—
  Round she trod the strain:
To right trod she—to left trod she,
  And trod all o'er again.

XXXVIII.

Till wearied out, her tender frame,
　By longing hope deferred,
She sank down on the spot—the same
　Where first the tune she heard.

XXXIX.

As though her mother Earth would bear
　Some comfort to her dearth,
As Indian catches in his ear,
The presence of some mortal near,
　By listening to the earth.

XL.

And thoughts rose up within her lips,
　To tell what anguish wrung
Her heart, but fell, as fountain drips,
　Back to whence they sprung.

XLI.

For beat her heart so piteously,
　No word could dare essay,
To fill its grief, or sorrow dree,
　Or soothe its woes away.

XLII.

And as she lay, the song once more
   Burst in upon her swoon,
As the mystic fire that revels o'er
   The dismal-faced lagoon :

XLIII.

"Not in fields of clover,
   Neither in the bower,
Nor by rushing rover,
   But here, at this hour."

XLIV.

And as bright morning bursts from night,
   Sweet words escaped her gloom—
" And *I am here*, my Kevin dear,
   I'm thine unto the tomb."

XLV.

Her thought so spread her lifeless form,
   It shook her till she wake ;
And lo ! as sun o'er March cloud dun,
   Her love bounds o'er the brake.

XLVI.

And quickly raised was Eva fair,
　　Unto his sheltering heart;
And nestling there, as thought in speech—
The heaven she had pined to reach—
　　She prayed they'd "never part."

XLVII.

" And are you mine?"
　　　　　　　　" Thine, only thine!
　　Ay, darling youth, forever!
The earth holds not, so fair a lot,
　　That could me from thee sever!"

XLVIII.

" Oh, speak on yet—my Eva, yet—
　　Why should such sun-thoughts dally:"
" I am thine," she cried, " while the sky is blue,
Or the Dodder its Glan-nis-mole sings through;
While the seasons roll, and the loving birds
Warble to each their aërial words!
Though death should come, my love still true,
As the tree to the sod from which it grew—
While those darling hills—those elf-bound hills,
Embrace with calm shadows their offspring rills,

Or Kippure, like an aged parent fills
   The throne of state,
     With pride elate,
And fatherly views the valley!"

XLIX.

"Mine—*only* mine?"
          "Forever thine!"
And she clung around the youth
With the fervor which betrays itself,
   Supporting a woman's truth.

L.

He kissed her, and excess of joy
   So wrought, when strength had gone,
She felt that dizziness which doubts
   The fact one gazes on.

LI.

She felt as lifted from the sod
   Into his dear embrace—
But were it clouds her Kevin trod,
   She'd tread the self-same place.

7

LII.

Half waking from her swoon of heart,
　　She feels her in the air,
Mid myrial crowds that nimbly part,
　　To make her pathway there.

LIII.

Around, the sky—below, dim void—
　　And up she's onward driven:
'Tis a dream, like those her childhood enjoyed—
　　Dreaming of going to heaven.

LIV.

But round quaint little spectres flit,
　　Like motes in her bright splendor;
With jocund songs and gleeful wit,
　　And fragile shapes so tender.

LV.

And hither they run, and thither they run,
　　In vain their glee to smother;
And air looked a moving mine of gems,
　　As they pelt dew at each other.

LVI.

She clasped her arms about the youth,
　To feel had she been sleeping,
Full pure in confidence and truth,
　Of safety in his keeping.

LVII.

'Tis surely all some witching dream,
　Else her eyes need heart's upbraiding,
For Kevin, like the mist on stream,
　From her wild clasp is fading:

LVIII.

As shadow deftly fades away,
　When light approaches clearer,
Her opening gaze the maid betrays—
　No youthful Kevin's near her.

LIX.

The shape she prest to her maiden breast
　Has dwindled like a flower,
And left but a wizened, withered stem—
She sees the elves—she has heard of them.
Her whole life crowds in a frantic thought,
And crushes her as the truth is caught:

"Oh, hope belied—oh, Love," she cried,
"I have madly leased my soul from you,
While the Dodder runs and the sky is blue!"
    And swooned in the elfin power.

LX.

And wildly laughed imp Thatchet then—
    He roaring and running by fits,
Till e'en the elf-train, thought again and again
    He'd lose his elfin wits.

LXI.

Still alluring, still she follows
    In the love-struck elfin trance,
Far beyond the cloudy hollows,
    To where vagrant planets dance.

LXII.

Once they rested high in the blue,
    To school their wondering care;
And Time a lengthy cobweb threw,
    To teach her to walk the air.

LXIII.

In vast circles gathering round her,
　　As the systems round the sun,
Endless splendors hold, astound her—
　　Still beginning, never done.

LXIV.

Moving like vast seas of brilliants,
　　Each contributing its light
To the forming of a circle,
　　That shuts out forever Night.

LXV.

Still revolving, glittering onward,
　　High they chant a fairy glee,
As they pass, the echo, gone-ward,
　　Answers to her—" Who are ye ?"

(I.)

We are Faeries—gleesome Faeries!
　　From the 'haunted raths below;
We are Faeries—tricksy Faeries,
　　From the glistening peaks of snow,

7*

From the far hills to the valley,
　From the valley to the shore,
And from shore to shore we rally,
　Never less, and evermore !
　　　From the far light
　　　　Of Aurora,
　　　From the star-light
　　　　To the earth—
　　　From the sprye-lands
　　　　Of rich Flora,
　　　To the sky-lands,
　　　　We hold mirth !

(II.)

We may caper on the sunbeam,
　Or rest behind the moon,
When the pleasaunce of our night-dream
　Ushers in a lazy noon ;
We raise a monument of dew,
　Distilled from aërial flowers,
And joys like these are waiting you,
　And every charm that's ours.
　　　From the icebergs
　　　　Of the Vikings—
　　　From the spice-bergs
　　　　Of the East—

To the Prairies,
　　Are the likings,
For the Faeries'
　　Glorious feast!

(III.)

We may stretch a bridge from pole to pole,
　　Wing earth, and all that's in it,
Over the spheres, or round we can roll,
　　Or pass through in a minute.
We are Faeries—happy Faeries!
　　Giddy, tinted shades of dew:
Whose ever-bursting joy ne'er varies,
　　But to double—so shall you!
　　　　From the prismal
　　　　　Sun-light glory,
　　　　To the dismal
　　　　　Caves of earth—
　　　　From the Flood-god's
　　　　　Saga's hoary,
　　　　To the Wood-gods,
　　　　　Give us mirth!
We are Faeries—happy Faeries,
　　Kings of earth and sea and blue;
Whose ever-bursting joy ne'er varies,
　　But to double—so shall you!

LXVI.

"I fecks you will," quo' Thatchet.   "True!
    And if you hest have a mate
Like me," and he kissed young Daisy-dew,
    Who dealt him a box on the pate.

LXVII.

Eva was listless of all earth,
    Enchanting her promised dower;
And her eyes are tinct with elfin dew,
    To give her sight elfin power.

LXVIII.

And soon with the rites of Elfin Land
    They shrive the maid from clay;
And she, in the joy of the fairy band,
    Is not less gay than they.

LXIX.

She revels along as though she ne'er
    Was born out o' the blue,
And floats athrough the loving air,
    Scarce knowing she passes through.

LXX.

And joyously down the azure space,
    They sweep like a stellar shower,
To meet the Queen at the gathering place,
    By the Brocken o'er Alyagower.

PART FIFTH.

I.

Young Kevin went to the ruin gray,
  Quilted in ivy green,
Where yestere'en his love did pray,
  And Eva's had plighted been.

II.

The young oak branches sighing, bow'd,
  The weird yew wept aghast,
And the ivy leaves, a clustering crowd,
  Shivered as he passed.

III.

The sad old ruin lonely stood,
  A solemn sight to see,
Like one who suffering for his love,
  Longs from the earth to flee.

IV.

Yet there it stood mid the solitude,
    And the wave-like graves so dim,
A beacon rock midst the ghostly flock,
    Beloved unto him.

V.

For to him it brought thoughts of love,
    Of purpose high and pure :
He thankful felt to heaven above,
    And on the earth secure.

VI.

Beneath its calm and holy shade,
    His kindling heart had burned,
And blazed, and spread, until the maid
    Its every glow returned.

VII.

And who, though frosted o'er by Time,
    Or varied fortune, can
Forget the place, where woman's grace
    First made him feel a man.

VIII.

What heart that does not hold the scene,
  As heaven's foretaste here;
The purest, best, that eyes caressed!
  Beyond all others, dear?

IX.

God pity him whose peevish fate,
  Or thoughtless, callous ways,
Cannot with such remembrance mate
  Sweet comfort, bliss, and praise.

X.

And can we wonder Kevin thrilled
  With feelings strangely new,
Where Eva's yearning bounty filled
  The hopes that burned him through.

XI.

The echoes of her blessed voice
  In spreading sounds still seethed
Around the spot, and the youth's heart caught
  So tightly, he scarce breathed:

XII.

Lest with the breathing he might fail
    To catch each fancied tone,
That bade him a life-pathway hew,
    Wide and bright enough for two,
        Nor henceforth be alone.

XIII.

The scene, the sounds, the hopes did span
    The youth; till past control
Their mingling pleasures over-ran,
    The chalice of his soul;

XIV.

And burst forth into frenzied speech
    Which he could not suppress:
But what are words to teach, or reach
    The wants of happiness?

XV.

"Ah, happy me! O chosen one,
    Thy fasting eyes prepare,
To feast their hungry glances on
    Thy life-absorbing fair!

XVI.

" Ah, happy me! O proudest one!
    Restrain thy throbbing side :
It swells amain with radiant pain
    Till comes thy radiant bride."

XVII.

Ah, well-a-day, and wo is me,
    That hath this tale to tell :
Would that the elves had left me free
    To break the fairy spell.

XVIII.

The while young Kevin Dhu devoured
    His brain with hopeful bliss;
The gloaming fled, by night o'erpowered,
And the long grass on the dim graves cowered
    Beneath the dew's cold kiss.

XIX.

A shaking off love's lethargy,
    That captive held each limb,
The doubts and tears, of passion's fears,
    In a torrent burst o'er him.

XX.

He wandered up, he wandered down,
  He counted every tomb;
They seemèd with a ghoulish pith
  But mimicking his doom.

XXI.

Which way he turned—each tomb he read,
  Held nothing to his eye,
Save these huge hopeless words of dread—
  "Sacred to Memory."

XXII.

With startling apathy he took,
  His eyes from death and clay,
And up into the heavens did look,
  For some heart-easing ray.

XXIII.

But as to chill his fibres through,
  And warn his aching sight,
A black cloud, like a hand, came o'er
  And hid the eye of night.

XXIV.

The weary, sad, suggestive tombs,
  The black and dreary cloud,
The trees like beck'ning funeral plumes,
  The ivy like a shroud;

XXV.

The Dodder's cloud-affrighted waves,
  A moaning, stealthily past,
The winds that wail down the crooked vale
  And burst into gusts at last:

XXVI.

Conveyed to him a weakening sense
  Of desolation near,
Till he scarce could gasp 'neath the icy grasp
  That crushed his heart with fear.

XXVII.

He thought he heard upon the air,
  Around the ruin dim,
Strange voices mutter as in prayer,
  And say—"God pity him."

XXVIII.

His eyes were fraught with helpless power,
　　Into the dark saw he;
And he read as plain as at noonday hour—
　　" Sacred to Memory."

XXIX.

The Cross, as one with outstretched arms
　　And head to heaven, did seem
To tell him that 'gainst charms and harms
　　Of earth it was supreme.

XXX.

Upon the youth's bleak ashen heart
　　This holy thought did move
The embers, till there leapt apart
　　The flames of Faith and Love.

XXXI.

The dark distempers of his brain
　　Before his Faith rushed out—
" Oh, dearest love, she'll come again,
　　Why—why should I e'er doubt."

XXXII.

" To-morrow I will clasp my fair
    More bright than mountain fay !"
The sky became more overcast,
He shivering Saint Anne's Well past,
The winds grew wild, more black the sky,
And the shaggy trees, as he went by,
In mournful dirges called him back ;
But he held on his lonely track,
    Sighing, saying, " Fairest fair,
    More bright than mountain fay !"
And he took himself, though loth to part,
From the spot so dear to his hopes and heart,
    And homeward bent his way.

XXXIII.

Days, and weeks, and months, and years,
    Passed over, and the youth
Still paced the place of love and tears,
    Where he had pledged his troth.

XXXIV.

He there might pace till Judgment-day,
    Pace he might for ever,
For her he sought in the ruin gray,
    Again on earth stood never.

XXXV.

Beneath the Cross in that ruin gray,
  The tombs right fronting where
IIis Eva sat, his manhood's day
  Passed, talking to the air.

XXXVI.

And oft he played his harp and sung
  The rhymes he used to sing,
And oft her name was on his tongue
  In senseless wandering.

XXXVII.

And when at deep sun-set he played
  Some plaintive air she loved,
He thought the rocks and woods betrayed
  A feeling, and were moved.

XXXVIII.

The hills seemed leaving the dreary posts
  They had sentinelled for ages,
And the ravines aroused their minstrel hosts
  To march with their chiefs and sages.

XXXIX.

To him the vales more wide did gape,
   The Dodder dull had grown,
All things seemed longing to escape
   From him, save the Cross alone.

XL.

And Kevin at its base grown old,
   A life of calm wo passed,
To it he clung, his silent, strong,
   And true friend to the last.

XLI.

Of years threescore, and more, had fled
   Since he with joy nigh dumb,
Went forth to meet his Eva sweet
   And still, he thinks, she'll come.

*   *   *

XLII

It is a glorious close of day :
   In light and shade the rills
Gleam fondly in the ruddy ray,
   That nears the western hills.

XLIII.

In smiles of light, the heath, the rocks,
  Slantwise the sun-beam kissed,
And rested on old Kevin's locks
  Of tangled silver mist.

XLIV.

Anticipating twilight's frown,
  It came by Mercy led,
And wove a supra-mortal crown
  Around old Kevin's head.

XLV.

His spectral fingers o'er the strings
  In trembling labor went;
The minstrel and the minstrel's wings
  Of song, are nearly spent.

XLVI.

Beneath the friendly Cross his soul's
  Dear cause he whisp'ring pour'd;
But sighs like his are organ rolls
  To the ear of Mercy's Lord!

XLVII.

As one who yearns to live alway,
  Eastward he turned his eyes,
With hopes to see from the night of clay
  Eternal dawn arise!

XLVIII.

His night fell on him as he gazed,
  Ere the sun had wholly fled,
And the sun-crown shone—Oh, God be praised!
  O'er the lover-minstrel—dead.

XLIX.

On the spot where he love's passion drank,
  On the gray and wiry moss,
And leaning on his harp, he sank
  In the shadow of the Cross.

NOTES.

1. "Delightful Glan-nis-mole."

—Part I., verse xvi., p. 11.

Glan-nis-mole, or the Vale of Thrushes, a peculiarly wild, romantic, and picturesque valley in the Dublin mountains. Kippure, the highest of this range, lifts its brown head over all the neighboring hills, at the remote end of the valley. On it the river Dodder takes its rise from three springs, which join a short way down, and thence united, springs into the vale, and commences its wild and devious course. The writer tracked the river to its source, and explored the surrounding hills and glens twenty years ago. The

"Ivy-quilted scanty ruin"

(stanza xxiv.) then standing, was the remains of a primitive Christian church, on the right bank of the Dodder. On the opposite bank the rugged hills and table-lands of Alyagower, Kiltipper, Ballymanock, and the yet more wild Castlekelly, are variously prominent. The "Witched Cornaun," one of the Dublin range, better known as the old hill of Rollinstown, and at present called Montpelier, lies to the northeast of Kippure As suggested by the name, Glan-nis-mole was famous for thrushes, and has been distinguished as the scene of some poems attributed to Ossian. The title of one of these is, "The Lay of the Tall Woman from beyond the Sea, or the Hunt of Glan-nis-mole."

9

2. " The sunbeam is shed, through a rose-leaf, red
   On a neighboring ceanavaun."

—Part I., verse xxxiv., p. 15.

The ceanavaun, a wild plant, the top of which bears a sub-
stance somewhat resembling cotton, and as white as snow.

3. " These crosses, like great note-marks, stand

  * * * * *

Referring us to God."

This metaphor was suggested by J. [De Jean] Fraser's lines—

" The stars are asterisks in Heaven,
 Referring us to God."

4. " His love was fierce as St. Kevin's hate."

—Part I., p. 22.

The legend of the persistent passion of the fair Kathleen for
St. Kevin, and his equally persistent abhorrence of her attention,
even to hurling the lovely votaress into the waters of Glenda-
lough, will be remembered by readers of Moore's Melody—" By
that Lake whose gloomy shore," and Gerald Griffin's ballad,
" The Fate of Cathleen."

5. " His tongue seemed in his fingers."

—Part I., verse lxxiii.

The expression of the hands, in either delight, hate, agony, or
scorn, is most powerful. In Raphael's cartoons, especially in
Paul Preaching at Athens, The Death of Ananias, The Sorcerer
Struck Blind, we can see the wonderful effect of the expression
of the fingers. They are all speaking, and in the words of
Shakspeare one may exclaim—·

" I *see* a voice !"

The subject is too suggestive to be more than indicated in a note

6.   "the mystic Well,
Blessed by the good Saint Anne."

—Part II., verse x., p. 33.

In a previous ballad by the writer " Saint Anne's Well" has
been described. A brief extract will be sufficiently explanatory
of the allusion in the text:

"The waters are clear and as pure as the soul
  Of the Saint that endowed it. Beneath a green knoll
It peacefully slumbers in hallowed repose,
And though always brimming, it never o'erflows;
For a side-long trickle leads off the blest flow,
When its breast is too full, to the Dodder below;
And skirts by the little church Kilmosantan,
Where the green ivy close the old ruin doth span,
And clings like a lover whose constancy wages
A war with old Time—growing fonder through ages!
On these lonely waters the Saint left a spell;
Which faith have the people, and thence to the well
They fly for its draughts; for the power Saint Anne
Bestowed on the spring was, that if mortal man
Was maimed, ill, but faith had, he'd surely get ease,
If he creep from the well to the church on his knees."

—" Faith and Fancy," pp. 69-70.

Its waters are deemed not less efficacious if they can be partaken
of by a purgatorial sufferer.

7. " Honey-tongue and Folks-glove."

—Part III., verse xvi., p. 45.

Folks-glove, the fairy, or wee folk's glove. The flower com
monly called fox-glove.

8. " And fairy scannachies with beards
    Of silver thistle-down."

             —Part III. verse xxiii., p. 46.

Scannachie, an ancient historian or story-teller.

9 " And all ye that wraithe Glancree,
    Or guard the lonely haunted Loughs."

             —Part III., verse xxxiv., p. 50.

Glancree, a wild and eminently romantic locality. The loughs alluded to are the contiguous lakes, but which are known as " Lough Bray." There are two, the upper and lower. The latter is the more picturesque. It is wild and solitary, situated up in the mountains, and presents evidence warranting the belief that it is the crater of an extinct volcano. The fairies have great repute hereabouts

Second Edition of Savage's Poems.

FAITH AND FANCY,

BY JOHN SAVAGE,

AUTHOR OF "SYBIL," A TRAGEDY.

Notices of the Press.

Mr. Savage betrays the workings of an ardent, poetical temperament. He is always in earnest, often enthusiastic, and is never at a loss for language or imagery to express his feelings. . . . He makes a successful appeal to the love of nature and the love of country, and kindles sympathy with his expression of manly and generous sentiment.—*N. Y. Tribune.*

Will add to Mr. Savage's reputation for brilliancy of imagination, sweetness of fancy, and force of diction. . . . . "To an Artist" is a beautiful and solemn lyric, full of delicate and profound thought. . . . The "Washington" is the grandest and most exhaustive poem yet devoted to the Father of his Country.—*N. Y. Courier.*

Vigorous, patriotic, rhythmical, and many of them are marked with imaginative power. "The Muster of the North" is a bold and striking poem.—*Continental Monthly.*

There is one poem that, above all the rest, possesses a charm for us—that for its merits alone should insure immortality to the name of its author, and which we give in full, because it is intensely, entirely, and truthfully Irish in sentiment and inspiration. It is "Shane's Head," published many years since in the *Citizen*. There is a peculiar power and pathos observable in all the Irish poetry of this character, as all will remark who read such examples as the "Lament for O'Sullivan Beare," the "Lament for Patrick Sarsfield," and Davis's beautiful "Lament for Owen Roe O'Neil." All the best features of these are to be found in "Shane's Head," while

9*

in dramatic power and faithful portrayal of the stormiest gusts of human passion—grief, despair, hate, and desire for revenge—it transcends them all.—*Irish American.*

It does not contain a tithe of Mr. Savage's heart-utterings in song, but there is sufficient here to stamp him as a poet. He has that eager abundance of expression, that rich affluence of language, that passionate swelling of thought, determined to find melodious utterance, which, in union, make the poet. The grand lyric, "The Starry Flag," and that other spirit-swelling ballad of '61, entitled "The Muster of the North," which have found echoes in thousands of quick bosoms, lead off this collection. There are several other war lyrics, a magnificent Irish ballad ("Shane's Head"), and the poem upon Washington's portrait, which, originally published in *Harper's Magazine*, obtained great praise at the time. The characteristics of Mr. Savage's poems are earnestness, fire, melody, truth. His is not a cold, phlegmatic nature, which can calmly set itself down to the mere making of verses—it is impulsive, eager, productive, and *will* utter what it thinks.—*Philadelphia Press.*

Marked by a vein of tenderness and humane charity that speaks well for the heart of the writer, and unites him at once in sympathy with his reader. We quote an instance (A Battle Prayer) which breathes of the Christian as well as the Soldier. . . . . The two strongest poems in the volume are "The Starry Flag," and "The Muster of the North." The latter is a spirit-stirring, earnest, and admirably descriptive poem. It is a ballad of '61, and describes with wonderful vivacity and faithfulness, the "hurry," the indignation, the wild enthusiastic rush to arms, which followed the rebel firing upon Fort Sumter. It is a poetical history of one of the most exciting incidents in the most eventful period of the nation's existence.— *Watson's Weekly Art Journal.*

"The Dead Year" is replete with poetic imagery; "Snow on the Ground" is an exquisite gem. . . . . "At Niagara" is another poem of strength and beauty. Mr. Savage's writings partake of his spirit; he is an ardent lover of nature—the tiniest flower that blooms in the forest, or the grandest and most impressive of her monuments, alike inspire his poetic soul. He has a liberal nature, that blossoms into all human generosities at the sight of the Master's handiwork. Such natures make poets; they will be remembered, "growing fonder through ages," long after the poet's dust has mingled with its mother earth.—*Troy Daily Times.*

Replete with sentiment and pregnant with that sweet philosophy which seems to pervade all John Savage's rhythmical productions —*N. Y. Dispatch.*

Vigorous in conception, often strikingly original both in thought and diction, and in versification varied, but always melodious. Mr. Savage is indisputably a true poet.—*N. Y. Atlas.*

The author exhibits a signal imaginative and verbal power—embodying the fancy in the most apposite diction. . . . . . "Flowers on my Desk," "Mina," and "Dreaming by Moonlight," are perhaps the three gems of the book, and invite a repeated and grateful study. —*New Orleans Times.*

Mr. Savage inscribes his volume to the Hon. Charles P. Daly, in commendatory and affectionate appreciation of that gentleman's "generous efforts in behalf of Letters, Science, Humanity, and Justice"—and in the dedication lets us into the secret, doubtless, of the influences which inspire himself. He says that every person who writes poetry makes his reader the confidant of his hopes, woes, experiences, or sensations; for, he adds, "if he aspire at all to transcribe or embody the feelings which evoke or prompt human action, he cannot help writing largely from his own heart's blood, and in the hues it has taken by contact with Men, Faith, and Nature." This accounts for the subtle, sensitive, picturesque, and passionate character of many of the principal pieces in the work. They bear distinctive marks of being studious and philosophical observations of life and landscape, of art, men, and books, guided and illuminated by that insight which amounts almost to intuition, and gives the poetical mind its power over lesser organizations.

The "Muster of the North" has been widely copied and quoted. Taking it, not as an expression of political faith, but as an historical photograph of what the Count De Gasparin calls the great uprising, it has all the characteristics of the thrilling epoch. It throbs with emotion and commotion from the first line to the last, and sweeps you breathlessly along on its bounding measure. It is difficult to make an extract from it, the atmosphere of concentrated action so surrounds the whole. It is full of scenes for a Darley to illustrate or an Eastman Johnson to paint.—*Merchants' Magazine.*

John Savage's book of Poems, "Faith and Fancy," which is now far advanced in the second edition, has met a most favorable reception from the leading press of Ireland. The Dublin *Nation* devotes nearly a whole page to a review and many quotations. In the course of the article the critic says: "Of Mr. Savage's powers as a writer no one could doubt who had read the graphic pages of his ''98 and '48.' The breadth and freedom of those sketches, the close perception of character, and the dramatic force of the whole, gave promise for the author, which since then he has continued to realize. His recent work, 'Sybil, a Tragedy,' we know only through the critiques of the American press, which give it high meed of praise, and describe it as having proved a remarkable success on the stage. The little volume now before us consists of a number of poems contributed by the author to various American periodicals. Some of them have long been flitting about, in an anonymous, vagrant way, from journal to journal, brightening the 'Poet's Corners,' where they lit, like those gay-colored birds that give a flower *pro tem.* to every tree and shrub on which they rest; others, written since the outbreak of the war, and glowing with the patriotic excitement of the occasion, have received even a wider circulation." The *Nation*, strange to say, is lukewarm on the Union side of the American question, and thinks that however well Mr. Savage's National American lyrics " may reflect the popular enthusiasm, however effective they may be by the camp-fires or from the lips of recruiting-sergeants," they are of less beauty than those other compositions, in which " we get the more original ideas and the finer expressions of a 'poet born, not made.' " " The War Songs," it says, " may be the more popular now in America—the others will live longer in the literature of the country." Among the specimens quoted are the " Requiem for the Dead of the Irish Brigade," " Game Laws," which has also been translated in Germany with honorable mention, " Breasting the World," some of the " Winter Thoughts," " Niagara," in which, says the *Nation*, " there are some fine thoughts, and such a measured march of rhythm and gravity of expression as well befit the subject;" " Mina, a pretty sketch, touched easily and brilliantly," and the stormy emotional ballad of " Shane's Head;" the critic concluding with this suggestive paragraph :

" The collection from which we have taken the foregoing pieces is not a large one, but poetry is not to be measured by bulk. Mr. Savage's writings show that he has preferred to be the author of a few pieces, with his own thinking in them, rather than give to the public a mass of common thoughts and common phrases, jumbled into rhyme. His " Faith and Fancy" will find favor with all admirers of genuine poetry."

The *Irishman*, of the same city, gives the book a hearty welcome, and singles out " The Muster of the North," " God Preserve the Union"—" a splendid poem, now heard by many a camp fire;" " A Battle Prayer"—" for its profound feeling and piety" (we gave it in the *Art Journal*); " The God-child of July"—" a beautiful birthday ode;" " At Niagara"—" opening grandly and well sustained throughout;" and " Shane's Head," which it thinks " too popular to need quotation," for special mention. The *Irishman* is enthusiastically on the side of the Union as against the rebellion of the South, and in these hearty words generalizes its appreciation of Mr. Savage's literary character:

"John Savage is already well known as an author. His 'Ninety-Eight and Forty-Eight' obtained considerable popularity; while his tragedy of Sybil acquired a degree of success that attracted the eulogiums not only of American but of English journals. Indeed, his genius seems chiefly adapted to dramatic writing, even more than to the lighter class of poetic productions. Into the lyrics contained in this volume the author has put his heart and soul, and made them instinct with vehement life. Many of them have already become classical; those, especially, which treat of the great crisis now convulsing America, have obtained popularity extensive as the poet's imagination. The poet sings the cause of liberty in America with the same sacred fervor which inspired him in Ireland."— *Watson's Weekly Art Journal, July* 23, 1864.

In Press, Library Edition,

SYBIL,

A TRAGEDY IN FIVE ACTS,

AS REPRESENTED AT

THE PRINCIPAL THEATRES OF THE UNITED STATES, BY AVONIA JONES,
MATILDA HERON, AND MRS. EMMA WALLER.

CRITICAL OPINIONS.

" This piece was originally produced at St Louis, with Miss Avonia Jones as the heroine, and successfully played by her for over sixty nights during that season, in Louisville, Chicago, Cincinnati, Richmond, New Orleans, and the other principal cities in the South and West. She afterwards appeared in California and Australia, and was everywhere received in this character with enthusiasm. She was almost invariably called before the curtain after the third, fourth, and fifth acts of the play, and on one occasion the excited audience followed her to her hotel, and would not disperse until she made her appearance on the balcony."—*Home Journal.*

" The play is well written—the language good, the dialogue easy, and the situations effective. . . . . It is of that domestic kind which is always popular, and is one of the best American productions we have seen."— GEORGE D. PRENTICE, *Louisville Journal.*

" The play of Sybil is one of no ordinary merit. With the exception of the introductory act, which seems to us to be tedious, and not suitably preparatory for the thrilling drama which follows, it is a tragedy which ranks with the immortal works of the best writers for the stage. There is nothing in the plays of Shakspere more beautiful and affecting than the scene in which *Sybil* asks an oath for the destruction of her seducer, and her lover kneels by her side, and looks to heaven and takes the terrible oath."—*Louisville Courier.*

" The story is of well-sustained interest throughout, and the plot well handled by the dramatist. The three last acts will well compare with any dramatic product on the modern stage. . . . ."—*Richmond Enquirer.*

" Mr. John Savage's play, 'Sybil,' was produced at the St. Charles last night before a large auditory, from whom it received a triumphant reception. As an acting drama it has points of effect which will keep it upon the stage when the actress for whom it was written shall walk the boards no more. Though often trembling on the very brink of the blood and thunder abyss of the melodrama, it is constantly rescued and assured to respectability by the purity and loftiness of expression, and by the unexpected *denouements* of the minor complications. The staple of the plot is of a nature so delicate as to require the most gingerly handling, and we confess that we were surprised and pleased by the skilful manner in which the dramatist has managed it. The minor scenes are discreetly made only so long as is necessary to the continuity of the plot. The part of *Sybil* is a study, for it is the most *natural* unnatural character that we can recall in the range of the drama. As to its performance, we never saw Miss Jones in any other part approach to the tragic power she displayed in this."—*New Orleans Daily Crescent.*

"This production. having created quite a sensation in the several cities in which it has been put upon the stage, excited more curious interest among our playgoers than any other dramatic piece that has yet appeared upon the bills. . . . . . . As a production of high literary merit there is no question of its claims. It is, perhaps, unequalled among the more modern productions."—*Memphis Avalanche.*

"The genius of the author rises in grandeur with the stirring incidents of the scenes that rapidly succeed each other, from the commencement of the third act to the close of this thrilling drama of domestic life."—*San Francisco National.*

"The Play of 'Sybil' is beautifully written. Many of its passages are poetic gems. It is replete with elegant diction, exquisite pathos, and soul-ennobling thoughts and expressions. It is almost too brilliant."—*Sacramento Dem. Standard.*

"Mr. John Savage's drama of 'Sybil,' which has acquired an historic interest, not only from the tragic episode on which it is founded, but from the circumstances attending its first production at the Louisville theatre, was brought out at this establishment (Winter Garden) last night. With such materials as Mr. Savage had to deal with, he could not well write a piece that would fail in interest; but there was for this very reason a fear that he would fall into the error to which all young playwrights are exposed in dealing with such a subject—that of investing it with a melodramatic character.

"That danger he has happily avoided. From the commencement to the close the effects are legitimate and owe but little to dramatic artifices. The language, though what might be expected from an accomplished writer, is never stilted or high flown, as first efforts of this sort are liable to be. The intensely absorbing interest of the main incidents might, it is true, have been relieved by a few broader dashes of humor in the characters of the inferior personages of the piece, and a little more local color might have been given to it; but, perhaps, on the whole, Mr. Savage exercised a wise discretion in confining himself to effects of which he was sure, and which, as the result proved, were amply sufficient for success.

"There is much to criticise, much to find fault with, in Miss Heron's impersonation of the character; but, with all this, it must be admitted that it was a remarkable performance. . . . . In the interview with ——she was really fine, reminding one at times, in the concentration of hatred and loathing which she exhibited towards him, of Rachel."—*New York Herald.*

"Last evening, she—Matilda Heron as *Sybil*—was in her highest form, and in the surge of sentiment and pomp of passion which swells around the character, she surpassed herself. . . . ."—*New York Daily Times.*

"Grand as she undoubtedly is in *Camille*, in the *Sybil* she quite eclipsed that character. The author has surrounded her with every variety of tender passion, revenge. and remorse, and each aspect of these varied feelings was rendered by Miss Heron in a manner not artistic, but life-like . . . . . The play may be set down as a great success."—*New York Express.*

"Upon these incidents, fresh and terrible as they are, Mr. John Savage has constructed a tragic drama. The author, albeit unused to the boards, has not fallen into turgidity. He has maintained a rare moderation of tone, looking to the fierce facts to sustain him. All that he portrays, and more, actually happened. When the villain meets the heroine in the play, she relents from her determination, and, while spurning his audacious advances begs him to fly, to escape her husband's wrath were he to find out his real name and character. This, as we have shown, is not in the real story. But it improves and varies the characteristics of the central figure; portrays feminine tenderness, which is the allurement of all women on or off the stage."—*New York Tribune.*

"She—Mrs. Waller as *Sybil*—was honored by being called before the curtain four times."—*Philadelphia Evening Bulletin.*

www.ingramcontent.com/pod-product-compliance
Lightning Source LLC
Chambersburg PA
CBHW020807060726
47498CB00017B/914